The messenger galloped up in a swirl of dust.

It was Good Friday, 1483, shortly before the hour of Nones, and the Gloucester household was picnicking beneath a stately weeping willow on the banks of the River Ure. Anne tensed and held her breath, then heaved a sigh of relief, for he did not wear the royal blue and wine livery of the King but a topaz tunic and the badge of the Black Bull. It was from Lord Hastings that he came. She took a bite of marchpane. But her happy munching slowed when he drew close enough for her to see his face.

Something had happened.

The man looked more than travel-worn. He looked deeply troubled and weary to exhaustion. He bowed to Richard. "My Lord Duke, I am the bearer of grievous tidings…" He paused, seemed to brace himself. "Your Grace… I deeply regret to inform you, the King is dead."

All laughter died; the minstrels ceased their song. Katherine, picking lilies at the water's edge, straightened. Johnnie, Ned, and young George Neville, playing knights and crusaders on the ruins of a stone wall, halted in their steps, and others, in the motion of setting down a game of cards, stilled their hands. Francis turned, his fishing rod limp, and from where he sat on a blanket, Richard stared mutely up at the messenger with unnatural stillness.

It is a tableau I will always remember, Anne thought.

The Rose of York:
Crown of Destiny

SANDRA WORTH

END TABLE BOOKS

Reviews and Awards

Crown of Destiny is the second book in *The Rose of York* series, winners of numerous awards.

> "Worth has done meticulous research... Though conversations and some incidents must of necessity be invented, she makes them seem so real that one agrees this must have been what they said, the way things happened."

> — Myrna Smith, Ricardian Fiction Editor, *The Ricardian Register*, quarterly publication of the U.S. Richard III Society, Vol. XXIII. No. 2

> "This powerful book, impeccably written, with its tender love story and brilliant analysis of Richard III's legacy, convinced me that Shakespeare completely misjudged this remarkable King who reformed the jury system. Not since *Atlas Shrugged* have I been so deeply moved."

> — The honourable Ramona John, author and judge.

The Rose of York: Crown of Destiny won the 2003 Royal Palm Literary Award of the Florida Writers Association. As part of *The Rose of York* series, it also won First Place in the Historical/Western Genre of the 2000 Authorlink New Author Awards Competition, judged by top New York agents and editors, and swept all nine categories to win the Authorlink Grand Prize.

Acknowledgements

My thanks go to my publisher for the tireless care given to this manuscript, and to fellow Metropolis Ink author and friend Wendy Dunn, who was instrumental in seeing it through to press. I am also grateful to the Richard III Society, particularly Roxane Murph and Myrna Smith, for their assistance.

This book could never have been written without the support of many friends, new and old. Three whose support knew no limits and who contributed to this book in more ways than can be mentioned here are my agent, Irene Kraas; noted graphoanalyst Florence Graving; and my childhood friend Dr. Dolores Drysdale of Toronto, Canada, whose wisdom has been the rod on which I have leaned these many decades. Each has earned my lifelong gratitude and I stand forever in their debt. Dale Summers, with whom I shared my first Ricardian tour of Britain before any thought of a book was born, has acted as advisor and cheered me on during the ten years I spent writing this series. To Dr. Barbara Low, who enriched my life with laughter, I owe a debt of thanks for her loving and staunch support over many years and many lattes. No mention would be complete without Professor Dagobert Brito, who provided encouragement throughout this endeavour. Special thanks also go to Linda Shuler and the honourable Judge Ramona John, two of the most gifted writers I have ever known, and with whom I am proud to share membership in the "Late Bloomin' Roses Society." Finally, I wish to thank Moira Habberjam of Yorkshire, England, and the members of the Yorkshire branch of the Society whose friendship over ten years and enormous generosity has made a difference, not only to me personally, but to the research that went into the writing of this book.

Table of Contents

Historical Characters

In a tumultuous era marked by peril and intrigue, reversals of fortune and violent death, the passions of a few rule the destiny of England and change the course of history...

Richard: Distinguished by loyalty to his brother the King, and a tender love for his childhood sweetheart, he has known exile, loss, tragedy, and betrayal. But his loyalty is first challenged by war, then by the ambitions of a scheming Queen. Time and again he must choose between those he loves until—in the end—he is left no choice at all.

Edward: A golden warrior-king. Reckless, wanton, he can have any woman he wants, but he wants the only one he can't have. When he marries her secretly and makes her his Queen, he dooms himself and all whom he loves.

Bess: Edward's detested and ambitious Queen. Gilt-haired, cunning and vindictive, she has a heart as dark as her face is fair.

George: Richard's brother. Handsome, charming, and consumed with hatred and greed, he will do anything it takes to get everything he wants.

Warwick the Kingmaker: Richard's famed cousin, maker and destroyer of kings. More powerful and richer than King Edward himself, he attracts the jealousy of the Queen and seals his fate. (Deceased as this story opens.)

Anne: The Kingmaker's beautiful daughter. She is Richard's only love; his light, his life...

John: The Kingmaker's brother. Valiant and honourable, he is Richard's beloved kinsman and Edward's truest subject, but when the Queen whispers in the King's ear, he is forced to confront what no man should have to face... (Deceased as this story opens.)

This book is dedicated to my daughter Emily.

"O Fortune
variable as the moon,
always dost thou wax and wane."

— *Carmina Burana*: Songs from the
Manuscript Collection of Benedictbeuren

"Far off a solitary trumpet blew,
Then waiting by the doors, the war-horse neighed."

— *Idylls of the King*, Alfred Lord Tennyson

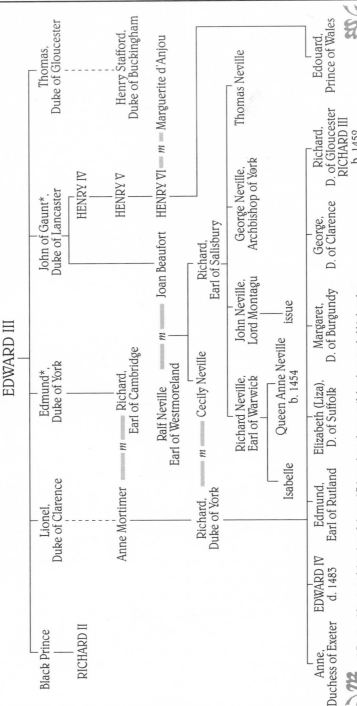

Introduction

Much has been written about Richard III, and many readers are familiar with Shakespeare's portrayal of him as England's most reviled and villainous monarch. What is not as widely known is that Richard III gave us a body of laws that forms the foundation of modern Western society. His legacy includes bail, the presumption of innocence, protections in the jury system against bribery and tainted verdicts, and "Blind Justice"—the concept that everyone should be seen as equal in the eyes of the law. He was also the first King to proclaim his laws in English so that poor men could know their rights, and the first to raise a Jew to England's knighthood.

Such ideas were revolutionary in the fifteenth century. They alienated many in the nobility and the Church, and played no small part in Richard's ultimate fate.

Two hundred years later, when it was safe to do so, men questioned the traditional view of Richard bequeathed to them by the Tudors and found themselves unable to reconcile the justician with the villain, the man with the myth. In the early twentieth century, such men came together to form the Richard III Society.

Two of Richard's most well known contemporary critics, Alison Weir and Desmond Seward, subscribe to Shakespeare's depiction of him as a hunchbacked serial killer. In his book *Royal Blood: Richard III and the Mystery of the Princes,* Bertram Fields, a prominent U.S. attorney and author, examines the school of thought represented by Weir and exposes the inconsistencies and deficiencies of the traditional view.

Richard III caught my imagination when I saw his portrait at the National Gallery, London. Then I read Josephine Tey's *The Daughter of Time.* This compelling mystery inspired me to consume whatever I could find on Richard and to make several research trips to England and Bruges in search of the true Richard. It was in Paul Murray Kendall's *Richard The Third* that I finally found him. Kendall, a Shakespearean scholar and professor of English Literature, provides a most convincing and illuminating portrayal of Richard and his times, and it is his interpretation of events that is reflected in this book.

While Shakespeare was a great dramatist, he never claimed to be a historian. In an age of torture and beheadings, he wrote to please the Tudors. The authority Shakespeare drew on was Sir Thomas More's *History of King Richard III*, a derisive account, which More never finished, of the last Plantagenet King.

An enduring mystery is why More broke off in mid-sentence and mid-dialogue to hide his manuscript. Fifteen years after his death, it was found by his nephew, translated from the Latin, and published. Had Sir Thomas More discovered the dangerous truth?

The questions remain, and the debate continues.

What Went Before...

Crown of Destiny is the second book in *The Rose of York* series, following *Love & War* and preceding *Fall from Grace*. Each book in the series is self-contained and may be read without reference to what went before, or what is to come. Each book has won its own individual pre-publication awards without the judges being aware that the book they were reading was part of a larger series. However, for those readers who are coming to this part of the epic saga that makes up the Wars of the Roses without knowledge of the first book in the collection and who would like to know what went before, and also for those readers of *The Rose of York: Love & War* who would like a re-telling of that story, I present a synopsis here.

Commencing in 1452, the Houses of York and Lancaster began their feud for the Crown of England. Each side chose the rose as their emblem; York chose the white, and Lancaster the red. Against this turbulent backdrop of the Wars of the Roses, the orphaned nine-year-old Richard Plantagenet goes to live with his famed and much older Yorkist cousin, the Earl of Warwick, nicknamed "Kingmaker." There he meets his cousin Anne Neville, daughter of the Kingmaker. Brought together in the Kingmaker's household as children, Richard and Anne grow up and fall in love. But thanks to Edward's avaricious and detested Queen, Elizabeth Woodville, a commoner whom King Edward had wed in a scandalous secret marriage, tensions between Richard's brother, King Edward IV, and Anne's father, the Kingmaker, erupt into war in 1471. Richard is faced with an agonising decision: does he choose his adopted family, the Nevilles, and his childhood sweetheart, Anne, or does he remain faithful to his vows of fealty to the King and choose his brother Edward?

He chooses to remain loyal to his brother King Edward IV. The House of Neville falls. Two of the three Neville brothers whom Richard had loved are slain at the Battle of Barnet, where they fought for the Lancastrian side. The third, an Archbishop, is imprisoned by King Edward in the Tower of London.

Meanwhile, Richard's brother George, who is married to Anne's sister, Bella, is spared Richard's anguish by the nature of his character: in any dilemma, George always chooses George. At first this means siding with Warwick the Kingmaker against his own brother King Edward. Later it means betraying his father-in-law, the Kingmaker, and rejoining his brother King Edward.

After war's end, George stirs up trouble for his brother Richard. Finding their union thwarted by George, Richard and Anne elope and are wed by Anne's uncle, the Archbishop of York, who has been released from imprisonment in the Tower. Soon afterwards, however, the Archbishop indulges in treason again. This time King Edward sends him to a far harsher fate: the fortress of Hammes in Calais.

Despite the family squabbles, Richard and Anne manage to find moments of happiness together. As *Love & War* closes, they welcome a child into the world and name him Edward, in honour of the King, Richard's brother. The cruel past seems far behind them. But they cannot guess how violently Fortune is about to turn her capricious Wheel once again...

CROWN OF DESTINY

1476–1483

Chapter 1

"Strike—strike—the wind will never change again."

T he ship rolled. Wine splashed the table. The small cabin filled with groans as men grabbed their cups.

King Edward IV laughed, saying, "Fear not. Soon there'll be plenty of free French wine!"

"Aye, Sire," grinned a knight seated further down the table. "Maybe we can drown the *Spider* in it." He leaned back and spat to emphasise the derogatory nickname of the French king, Louis XI. The knight peered down the table at a sallow-faced man sitting at the opposite end. "Or just slay him like a fish in a barrel, as we did the Bitch of Anjou's son at Tewkesbury, eh, Exeter?"

Henry Holland, Duke of Exeter, flushed and averted his eyes.

"Welladay, no need for that," said King Edward. "We're all friends here. My fair sister's husband may have been Lancastrian once, but he's Yorkist now, like the rest of us. Isn't that so, Harry?"

Exeter nodded nervously. "Aye, my Lord."

"And he'll fight as bravely for us in France as he did for Lancaster at Barnet, eh, Harry?" said the King, a smile on his lips that failed to reach his shrewd eyes.

"Aye, my Lord."

"See, what did I tell you, St. Leger? We're all friends here." King Edward grinned as he downed a gulp of wine and stabbed at a slice of venison with his dagger.

The hum of manly conversation resumed as the royal retinue returned lustily to their eating and drinking. But, though the knight's leer was gone, his face had hardened dangerously. While drinking his wine, he continued to glare at Exeter, who kept his own eyes fixed on his trencher. No one paid them any notice, except a dark-haired young man with deep grey eyes who sipped his wine thoughtfully.

The King's brother, Richard, Duke of Gloucester, let his gaze move from the knight, St. Leger, to the duke, Exeter.

Henry Holland, Duke of Exeter, was Richard's brother-by-marriage, wed to his eldest sister, Nan. Despite the marriage making Exeter a member of the Yorkist royal family, he had espoused the enemy cause during the civil war between the Yorkists and the Lancastrians and fled England when Yorkist Edward won the crown from the Lancastrian King Henry VI. After a decade abroad, he'd returned to fight against York. Captured at the Battle of Barnet, he'd languished in the Tower for five years, and had just been released by Edward's pardon.

So the rumours are true, thought Richard, his gaze returning to St. Leger. The knight's antagonism to Exeter was fuelled by a hatred more lethal than politics. St. Leger was enamoured of Exeter's wife—Richard's sister, Nan.

Welladay, it was bound to happen. No marriage could survive such a vast political divide—let alone a ten-year separation—unless there was love. Richard knew about such matters. His wife's father had been the leader of the rebellion against Edward's rule, and had fought, and died, for Lancaster. He also knew about jealousy. His wife had been wed to Henry VI's son, Prince Edouard of Lancaster.

Emboldened by wine, Thomas St. Leger spoke again on the subject he could not drop. "Sire, with your permission, I propose a toast. Let us drink to slaughtering the French like pigs in a pen, as we did the Lancastrians at Barnet and Tewkesbury! What say you, Exeter?"

Men snickered and eyes returned to the Duke of Exeter. A silence fell. As everyone watched, Exeter picked up his wine and emptied his cup. One by one the others upended theirs, exchanging winks as they drank.

Richard averted his gaze. The look in St. Leger's eyes as he had challenged Exeter was familiar. He'd caught it in his own too many times, for he, too, had once wished a man dead for the same reason. For an instant he wondered whether he would be taunting Prince Edouard of Lancaster if it were Edouard who sat in Exeter's place.

Yet strangely enough, it was Exeter who elicited his sympathy. He had never cared much for arrogant, swaggering St. Leger. Though a duke, Exeter had no allies, and no power or influence. He remained an outsider in an alien camp, resented by everyone.

Only under such circumstances could a peer of the realm be humiliated with impunity by a mere knight. Richard thought of his Yorkist cousin, John Neville, who had found himself in much the same circumstances, and had died fighting reluctantly for Lancaster at Barnet. Richard wondered if this was how it had been for John towards the end. Sudden anger swept him.

"St. Leger," said Richard.

The laughter died. Men's eyes turned to Richard.

"How is it that you, a former Lancastrian yourself—if memory serves me correctly—see fit to challenge a prince of the blood? Have you forgotten your own sympathies, as well as your station in life?"

St. Leger turned as red as the wine in his goblet.

"It seems to me that you owe my brother-by-marriage an apology."

Richard caught surprise in Exeter's gaze as he jerked up his head to look at him, and he also noted the bemused expression on Edward's face as he settled back to watch them. Richard returned his attention to St. Leger.

Fighting for composure, the knight took a moment before issuing his apology. "My Lord of Exeter. I meant no offence." St. Leger uttered the words through his teeth, a muscle twitching in his jaw.

"Louder, St. Leger. From where I sit, I can barely hear you."

The knight swallowed visibly, and a vein on his forehead throbbed, but he repeated his apology to Richard's satisfaction. Richard knew he'd made another enemy. But court was like that, and what was one more foe?

That night, in the royal cabin he shared with his royal brother and Edward's bosom companion, Lord William Hastings, Richard had trouble falling asleep. The seas were rougher than usual, and the talk of impending war with France had stirred painful memories. He tossed fitfully, trying to escape the images that rose before him: his cousin John Neville, in the fog of the battle at Barnet, halting in mid-blow to gaze at his Yorkist foe with grief-stricken eyes. John's brother, Warwick the Kingmaker, a lumbering, awkward figure as he fled the field in his armour, pursued by Yorkist soldiers who threw him into a river. Richard heard water splashing, then realized it wasn't water, but blood. Warwick turned his head, and Richard caught the look of anguish before his face was split in half by an axe and a tide of blood washed out the ghastly sight.

Richard groaned, turning away in horror, but the ghosts wouldn't let him rest. They scuffled in the dark and cried out for his help, their pleas muffled by the fog and the armour, by the din of battle and the screams of the dying. *No,* he moaned, *don't kill Warwick— don't kill John—not John, I pray you, not John...!* He heard someone laugh, and someone else say, "So may all Lancastrians end!" Then more laughter, and John appeared again, a strange smile on his face as he sank to his knees beneath the pounding of Yorkist swords and pikes.

Richard bolted upright on his pallet.

He was met by the sound of snoring from the other two beds where Edward and his boon companion Hastings slept. *I've been dreaming again.* He rubbed his eyes and threw back the covers, now too awake to sleep. Slipping on his boots, he grabbed his mantle. He creaked open the door and made his way along the dim passageway leading up to the forecastle. The lantern that hung near the ladder swung steadily, throwing shadows around him and triggering a childhood memory of a storm at sea, a tossing ship, and the tight grip of Warwick's hand on his own—a grip that had kept him from falling to certain death in the swirling black torrents below. He forced the memory away and grabbed the first rung of the ladder.

Drunken laughter drifted down from above. He looked up.

Flanked by two others, St. Leger was swaggering down, a broad grin on his swarthy face. "Somehow the very air smells cleaner now," he was saying to his friends. "What a fight he..."

St. Leger caught sight of Richard and his laughter was checked abruptly. The three men scurried back up the ladder and stepped nervously aside to make way. Richard passed them with a curt nod of acknowledgement, and turned to watch them disappear down the hatch, wondering vaguely what they had been up to.

The night was chilly for May. A wind had risen and the seas were choppy again. Richard pulled up his collar and grabbed the rope railing to steady himself. The skeleton crew that manned the ship was busy at the stern of the vessel. He moved to a corner of the bow, away from intruding eyes.

All was quiet. Peaceful. Only the sound of wind and water punctuated the cold, clear night. He looked up at the sky; a few frosty stars glittered in the heavens, radiating a sense of permanence.

But he knew that nothing was permanent, that life offered no certainties. He thought of his beloved wife, Anne, Warwick the Kingmaker's daughter, and his sweet babe, Ned, and wondered how they fared. Ned had been sickly since birth, and that worry had proved a greater burden than he and Anne would ever admit to one another. Never robust herself, Anne had suffered several miscarriages before Heaven had blessed them with Ned. The birth had been difficult, and the doctor had given him a choice: Anne's life, or the life of the babe. He had chosen Anne. By God's grace, they had both survived—but there would be no more children. So they doted on Ned, and fretted. His mind drifted back to their farewell in front of the castle walls.

"God keep you, my lady... and our fair babe," he had said as his eyes sought Ned. The little one had celebrated his first birthday the day before, the sixth of May, and now he slept in his nurse's arms, bundled tightly in the soft velvet blanket Anne had embroidered with his coat of arms of the Neville saltire and the Plantagenet Lilies and Leopards. His gaze moved to Anne's mother, Anne Beauchamp, Countess of Warwick.

She stood a step behind her daughter, looking matronly in the grey gown that flowed from her shoulders, her eyes sad beneath her soft hat and pleated veil. *How many times,* Richard thought, *had she stood as Anne does now, watching her own husband leave for battle, wondering if he will return?* "And you, Madame," he had said gently, "farewell. Guard them both for me till I return." She had inclined her head and given a small curtsy. He turned back to Anne.

Slender as a willow and radiant as a yellow rose, she stood in her robes and he was reminded of the first time they'd met, when she was seven and he was nine, and he'd thought he was gazing into captured light. Tears rolled down her cheeks now. Aye, parting held bitter memories for them both—the lessons of the past could not be forgotten, and at times like these, seemed too near for comfort.

He reached down and tilted her chin up to him. "All will be well, my sweet," he said. Anne's lips, fragrant and warm, brushed his.

A violent roll of the ship jolted him into the present. He grabbed the rope railing to steady himself. *Aye it's time to go back and give sleep another chance,* he thought. Fixing his gaze on the stars, he offered a prayer for their safekeeping, and that he would see them again.

~ ^ ~

At breakfast the next morning, Exeter was absent. Richard wondered how a man who had starved in the Tower for five years could miss a meal. When Exeter made no appearance at luncheon, Richard sent a man-at-arms to search for him. Then he went to join Edward in the cabin they shared.

Reclining against cushions, Edward looked up from the bed. Maps of France lay scattered throughout the cabin. He rubbed the back of his neck, and grinned. "I'm getting too old for war, Dickon."

"You'll feel better when you've won France," said Richard.

"Aye, it'll do my heart good, as well as my coffers. But if the truth be known, I'd rather be fighting the Battle of the Boudoir!" Edward laughed. "That's more to my taste."

Richard regarded his brother affectionately. That Edward preferred peace to war was well known and a trait widely regarded as a weakness. Many a plot against England had been hatched on French shores in the full belief that Edward's threats of reprisal would forever ring hollow. But genial as Edward was, much as he loved his pleasure, and though war interfered with the royal trade sending money flowing into his coffers of late, King Louis of France had troubled his peace too long. He itched to teach the French king a lesson.

With a slap to the thigh, Edward heaved himself up from the bed. "Welladay, the old *Spider* must be trembling now that I'm on my way to squash him, eh, brother? Remember what he said when he heard I would invade…" Edward placed his palms together, looked up at the sky, and mimicked in a squeaky voice, "Ah, Holy Mary, even now, when I have given Thee fourteen hundred crowns, Thou dost not help me one whit!" Edward roared with laughter.

Richard gave a tight smile. He himself had never cared for King Louis. Aside from the fact that Louis was a deceitful man and given to intrigue, Louis of France had been instrumental in arranging Anne's first marriage to Prince Edouard of Lancaster.

A knock came at the door. It was the man-at-arms Richard had sent in search of Exeter. "Your Grace, the Duke of Exeter is nowhere to be found."

"Are you certain?"

"Aye, my Lord. We've searched the entire ship. Even the latrine. There's no sign of him, and his pallet has not been slept on."

"Very well." Richard gave a nod of dismissal and waited until the cabin door had closed before turning to Edward. He found his brother watching him with a strange look in his blue eyes. Sudden realization struck him like lightning out of a clear sky. That was no dream he'd had the previous night! Murder had inspired it—or mingled with sleep to give his dream a hideous significance.

"Harry's dead, isn't he?" Richard said.

"Looks that way," replied Edward, toying with his empty goblet.

"What are you going to do about it?"

"Do?" Edward returned his gaze to his brother. "What am I supposed to do?"

"Find the murderers. Hang them."

Edward chuckled. "How unstatesmanly of you, Dickon. Don't you know I need all the murderers I can get to help me kill the French?"

Normally Edward's jests made Richard grin in spite of himself, but not this time. "You mean you're going to let St. Leger and his henchmen get away with this?"

"You don't know Harry was murdered. He might have fallen overboard. Or jumped."

The hint of amusement in Edward's tone angered Richard. "Pushed, more likely! Had I been a few minutes earlier going to the deck last night, I would have caught St. Leger in the act!"

"Perhaps, but you didn't. That leaves nothing but conjecture—not enough for which to hang a man."

"How can you be so unconcerned, Edward? For Christ's sake, a crime's been committed! Your prime duty as King is to serve justice."

"Ah, my little brother," sighed Edward, filling his goblet from a wine barrel in the corner, "you have always been overly concerned with the justice of the thing, haven't you? Heaven knows why." He downed a gulp and wiped his mouth with the back of his hand. "Look at the practical side for once, Dickon. Harry's no loss. He was a carved-in-stone Lancastrian. King Louis gave him succour those years of exile from England, and once we reached France he would have fled back into the Spider King's embrace the first chance he found... Taking our secrets with him, no doubt." He upended his cup.

Richard watched his royal brother drain his wine. Once upon a time, Edward had cared about justice as much as he did. But ensnared in his evil Queen's clutches, the golden, idealistic warrior-Prince had slowly degenerated into a King too fond of wine and women, concerned only with his ease—and the easy way out.

"Take my advice, little brother. Forget the whole unsavoury business. Harry's not worth it."

A rap came at the door. Edward's bosom friend Hastings entered, a genial smile on his broad-carved face. Richard inclined his head in greeting, trying to suppress his distaste for the man. Hastings was one of Edward's two debauched companions in his wantonness. The other was Edward's own stepson—the Marquess of Dorset, the Queen's son by her first marriage to Lancastrian knight Sir John Grey. With Edward's indulgence, Dorset had remained behind in England, ostensibly for the sake of his duties, but common knowledge held that cowardice, not duty, kept him there.

"Aha, Will, just the man I need to lighten my spirits! My little brother's heavy talk of murder and hangings has left me parched. Fetch yourself some wine and fill my cup while you're at it."

Richard realised that all further entreaties were useless. As he withdrew from the cabin, Edward called out, "Be happy for our sister, Dickon. She's free to wed St. Leger now. See, it turned out for the best after all!"

Chapter 2

"Lo, mine helpmate, one to feel
My purpose and rejoicing in my joy!"

Seated at the cradle, with her babe asleep at her shoulder and her faithful hound curled up at her feet, Anne Neville, Duchess of Gloucester, gazed out the window into the fading light of day. The gentle hills surrounding Middleham Castle glowed a deep green after the rain, and pear trees dotted the landscape with luminous white blossoms. Sheep bleated, and the church bells, never silent for long, tolled the hour of Vespers across the dales.

Day is already ending, she thought. How late it was. How quickly the seasons had flown! In this happy period of her life, time had a way of vanishing, and already the enchanted summer of 1474 that had brought her child into the world had yielded to the spring of 1475.

Servants entered to light the torches. She closed her eyes and nuzzled her sleeping infant, seeking strength from his warmth. Exhausted, she had taken a moment to rest from the endless stream of petitioners that filled the antechamber, but dismissing those who remained was out of the question. She could not turn her back on need. Once she had laboured as a scullery maid herself, and now, even her exalted status as Duchess of Gloucester failed to erase the memory of that desperate time in her life.

She took the sleeping child from her shoulder and laid him gently into his cradle. He stretched and gave a yawn. Anne smiled tenderly and adjusted his blanket with a gentle touch. Christened Edward, in honour of Richard's royal brother, the babe was a beautiful child, with Richard's dark hair and Neville-blue eyes that brought to mind her father, the proud Kingmaker, Richard Neville, Earl of Warwick. But it was the babe's dimples, which could only have come from her uncle John, Lord of Montagu, that caught the heart.

She smiled as she rocked his cradle. Reluctant to be parted from her little one, whom they affectionately called Ned, she used the nursery as a state chamber, giving orders to stewards and chamberlains, answering letters, arbitrating quarrels, and receiving petitioners. Her little Ned didn't seem to mind, and cooed or slept peacefully most of the time.

She felt a hand on her shoulder, and looked up from the cradle. "Let me dismiss them, my dear. Just this once?" said her mother, Anne Beauchamp, Countess of Warwick.

"No." Anne struggled to her feet. "I'm their only hope, Mother, or they wouldn't have made the arduous journey. You know I can't turn them away. Tomorrow there will be as many more."

"If George had not left me a pauper, I could help you," the Countess said.

The mention of George's name seemed to blow a cold wind into the room. Anne shivered. George was Richard's brother, who, after the civil war ended, had spitefully abducted her and hidden her away as a servant in a London kitchen so that she couldn't wed Richard. He had also stolen—there was no better word for it—her mother's lands and wealth, leaving her impoverished without even a roof over her head, and forced into Sanctuary. George had also tried to take Middleham Castle from them— Middleham, so full of memories, so much a part of them! She and Richard had met at her father's castle of Middleham when she was seven and he was nine, and they'd grown up to fall in love. Fortunately, Richard had won that dispute, and then invited the Countess to live with them.

"I know, Mother, but this is the way it is, and we must carry on as best we can. I just wish Richard hadn't left. I miss him so." She cast her sleeping babe a look of yearning as she tore herself from his side. Richard's absence ached in her heart as fiercely as it had during those terrible years when their families had been swept apart by war, but here, in this babe, lay solid remembrance of him, and a reminder that the fearsome past was dead.

It was a reminder she found herself needing constantly. She was secure now, happily wed to her childhood sweetheart, but the harsh memories of a past laden to the breaking point with loneliness, loss, and grief still rose up to torment her at odd hours of the day and night. Now that Richard had left for war, only little

Ned could chase away those dark memories and bring her comfort.

With a soft sigh, the Countess took Anne's place at the cradle. Delicate as her daughter was in appearance and in health, there was nothing delicate about her will. She would see the petitioners, every last one, and argument was futile.

Guessing the train of her mother's thoughts, Anne gave her an apologetic kiss on the cheek before moving to take up her stance at the centre of the dais. Heaving a sigh, Richard's old hound, Percival, followed her and arranged himself on her skirts.

Anne turned to a man-servant. "Ask Sir James to send in the nuns."

He withdrew with a bow. A moment later, the door opened and her steward, Sir James Tyrell, entered with a scrivener and two nuns in tow. The scrivener resumed his seat at his desk, Sir James stood beside him with a hand resting on the man's shoulder, and the nuns curtseyed, their habits crumpling to form two grey puddles on the bare floor. Anne bid them rise. "How can I help you?" she asked.

"I am from the Convent of Startforth," said one. "A boarder has come to us, Your Grace—an orphan. She is a deserving child, but without means. Her parents died of the plague and she has nowhere else to go, no family left. We cannot keep her without help, my lady. Times are hard, and we have barely enough to feed ourselves as it is."

Anne turned her gaze on the second nun.

"I am from the convent of Shildon, Your Grace. Our walls are crumbling. I come to beg a benefice to repair them."

"You shall both receive what you need," Anne said without hesitation. "Be it so noted, Sir James." Her steward nodded to the scrivener, who began scribbling. Anne gave her hand to be kissed.

"Thank you, my lady, thank you!" they cried in joyful unison. "May God bless you for your goodness, Your Grace. May the bounty of Christ be yours."

The nuns were ushered out. Other petitioners came and went: a poor knight seeking relief from his taxes, a prior who couldn't afford the fee for a royal licence, a free-holder whose sheep had died of disease and who needed a loan to get back on his feet. As the last one left the room, Anne was swept with a sudden bout of dizziness. The Countess leapt to her feet in alarm. Taking her daughter by the shoulders she led her to a chair.

"You shouldn't have gone to the village today! You're wearing yourself out, dear child. I keep telling you to stop visiting the sick— you're never been healthy, and whether you believe it or not, your charity in York can distribute food and clothing to the poor without you. But do you listen? No, you go and found another for the lepers..."

"Mother, you know why I do it," she managed, her voice a whisper. "The lepers are pitiful. And the poor are so happy to see me. How can I not go? It gives them comfort."

"Nothing you do is ever enough to stem the need. The sick and the poor and the desperate are always with us. Your charity will be the death of you!"

"Now, now, Mother," chided Anne, closing her eyes. It felt good to rest.

But she knew her mother was right. She'd set herself a cruel pace. Often, Vespers had passed and darkness had fallen by the time she could retire to the solar for a few precious moments with Richard and little Ned. But what joy in those moments! Sometimes she'd sing along with Richard as he played the lute for the little one, and sometimes she'd just sit, content to watch her mother bounce Ned in her lap. They all delighted in the simplest things he did. When Ned had smiled that very first time, it had seemed to her that the sun had risen at night...

There is joy in remembrance, she thought, her head clearing and calm settling over her as she came back to the present. She looked up at her anxious mother. "I'm fine, Mother. Truly. Whatever it was is gone now."

"Why do you drive yourself so, my child?" pleaded the Countess, concern evident in her eyes.

"Because I'm happy, Mother, and in my happiness I wish everyone happy."

"Your privy purse is drained making everyone else happy," she scolded, "while you scrimp."

"Yet there's nothing I'd do differently." Still a trifle dizzy, she went to the window seat and pushed the window open for air. The night was refreshingly cool, and a full moon shone in the dark sky. How she missed Richard! Edward had saddled him with such responsibility that they scarcely found leisure to admire the twilight or stroll in the moonlight together, as they had done when they were first wed. But despite his burdens, Richard was happy, too. She knew, because he called her "Flower-eyes" with ever-increasing frequency. Indeed, the castle glowed with joy and laughter, and like sunlight striking a mirror, the radiance reflected back on her. Now when she reviewed the past, she always paused at the wisdom of her decision in the abbey of St. Martin Le Grand—to elope with Richard and not wait for a papal dispensation.

Aye, love is all that matters. Love is everything. God understands, and will forgive. She had no doubts about that. Only one cloud marred her near-perfect horizon: little Ned was sickly. "Fret not, Flower-eyes," Richard constantly reassured her. "Remember that when I was small, I was always so near death that the steward in writing to my Lord father would add a postscript: 'Richard liveth yet.'" Then they'd laugh and turn their smiles on their child.

But the King's business took Richard away from Middleham far too often these days, and on those occasions when he was home, he was often preoccupied. For on his shoulders rested the weighty affairs of war and peace.

In the year since Ned's birth, Richard had accomplished wonders in York. His Council of the North, which he had set up to dispense justice to the poor, had grown into a body well-regarded by both rich and poor, righting many wrongs in the vast region under his control. And the border with Scotland, which was always troubled, had grown quieter. Thanks to his tireless efforts, England had secured a treaty and sealed it with the betrothal of James of Scotland's heir to Edward's five-year-old daughter, Princess Cecily. Even the seizure of English merchant ships on the high seas had eased. Other accords were also made, netting England peace with all her neighbours. All except France. With France, Edward had decided on war.

Anne remembered how Edward had laughed when he'd learned the French king's response to his proposed invasion: "I declare,"

Edward had said, wiping a tear of laughter from his eyes, "Louis's discomfort is such consolation, I am ready give up my bed for a soldier's pallet!"

No, Edward didn't care for war. The "Battle of the Boudoir" remained his passion of choice. *His lance always stands firm there,* she thought with a rare tightening of the mouth. Meanwhile, Richard toiled. It irked her that he didn't seem to mind Edward's failings. She still remembered how he had chuckled at Edward's missive. To raise money for the war, Edward had written that he'd been obliged to travel the realm and cajole his subjects for contributions. "What's so funny, my Lord?" she'd asked Richard as she'd made a game of dangling coloured baubles in front of Ned and snatching them away before he could grab them. She loved the sound of his giggles.

"A London dame offered Edward twenty pounds, and Edward thanked her with a kiss, whereupon she doubled her gift," Richard chuckled.

"Before, or after, the boudoir?" she had asked.

Engrossed in the letter, Richard had failed to rise to her bait. His brothers were the only subject they fought about and usually she tried to avoid giving offence, but sometimes things slipped out. She hated his adulation of Edward, whom she deemed unworthy of admiration.

"…All who went into their audience with frowns came out with smiles, wishing they could have given more to their king," Richard had continued, reading from the letter. "I vow Edward can pluck the feathers of his magpies without making them cry out. He jests with the people, embraces them, treats them as equals no matter how low-born, and wins their hearts. The soul is not born who can resist his charm! Edward expects to have the money by Easter."

"I shall take Ned for a stroll in the garden," Anne had said, rising abruptly, angry Richard could be so happy about the prospect of war. Did he care so little that she would be left behind to wait and worry? He gave no thought to her, only to Edward!

She bundled Ned tightly in his velvet blanket and gathered him up from the cot. Richard didn't notice her departure. At the door, she had paused, looked back. *Damn Edward.*

"Anne…"

Her mother's voice pierced her reverie. She blinked, startled.

"My dear, why so cross? What were you thinking about? Come away from the window; you'll catch cold. Let us go to the solar and read the missive Richard has sent. Nurse Idley will bring Ned."

In the solar, warmed by the flicker of numerous candles, wine, and the music of minstrels, Anne took a window seat with her mother while Percival stretched out to sleep on the Saracen carpet. Richard's news was not as good as she'd hoped. England's allies, who had promised Edward help against Louis XI, had so far failed to join them. Even Charles the Rash of Burgundy, who was wed to Richard's sister, Meg, had not come as he'd promised. They were still waiting for him, and increasingly fearful that they would have to fight the French alone.

She remembered the high promise of that day in May when Richard's battle cry had sounded across the dales of the North…

Horses neighed restlessly, plumes fluttered in the wind, and armour shone in the sun as Anne offered her husband the stirrup cup by the drawbridge of Middleham Castle. Clad in the white Milan armour he had worn into battle at Barnet, his dark hair stirring in the wind, Richard sat astride the magnificent white Syrian that Anne had chosen with King Arthur's white horse in mind to mark Richard's twenty-second birthday. *He looks his best on horseback,* Anne thought; a princely figure on a princely horse, though it required a firm hand to curb the restive stallion that whinnied with excitement, anxious to be off. Richard had become so devoted to the charger, White Surrey, that he rarely rode another. The spirited beast reciprocated the affection that had been won with gentle handling and many an apple and slice of marchpane.

Anne's proud gaze swept Richard's army. Men had answered his call to arms so willingly that he had found himself with three hundred more than he had promised Edward, and now the entire hillside blazed with silk-fringed banners of the White Boar.

"My Lord, I am not the only one who loves you. It seems all Yorkshire holds you in its heart," she said as he drank. Percival, standing by her sable-trimmed skirt, barked as if he, too, heartily supported the statement. Richard's gaze had followed hers to the ranks of plumes and bows waiting below the drawbridge.

"And that heart which was once Lancastrian is now Yorkist," he had smiled. Then, with a jerk of the bridle, he had turned his stallion and clattered over the drawbridge. Gloucester Herald had blown on his clarion, and the jewel-coloured cavalcade of plumes and banners had fallen in behind him and wound down the hill.

Anne rested the letter in her hand and made a fuss of Percival to hide the tears that suddenly blurred her vision. The thought that had filled her mind then was the same one that tormented her now: the last time she had sent a husband to war, he had not returned.

The Countess reached out and touched her sleeve gently. "My dear, it is our lot to wait and worry for our men," she said softly. "'Tis what women do."

"Aye, Mother. I wish to be strong, but sometimes… sometimes…"

The Countess squeezed her daughter's hand. "I know," she said.

Chapter 3

*"—but see thou to it That thine own fineness,
Lancelot, some fine day
Undo thee not."*

"**T**he curse of God be on the fool!" Edward fumed, pacing to and fro in his tent on the banks of the River Somme near St. Quentin. "We came all this way, and Charles, instead of preparing his forces for our grand assault on Louis as he promised, marched east to besiege Neuss!" He turned flashing eyes on his council. "Neuss, for God's sake. No one in his right mind cares about Neuss! He must be mad."

From his seat at the end of the plank table, Richard watched Edward, thinking how much he resembled a magnificent, fearsome, angry lion. At thirty-two he had put on weight, his hair had dulled, and his skin had loosened. But his blue eyes were as brilliant as ever and he exuded majesty in the set of his powerful shoulders, the stride of his long legs. If his hair was no longer the gold of youth, it was tawny as a lion's pelt, and if his brow was etched with lines, it was so nobly carved that it demanded a crown.

He looked around the royal tent. They were all watching Edward: their brother George; their sister's husband, the Duke of Suffolk; the Queen's brother, Anthony Woodville, Earl Rivers; Edward's good friend William Hastings; and his lords, which included ever-faithful Jack Howard and the slimy bishop, John Morton. Most slumped around the table, but Hastings lounged against a tent pole with folded arms, while the fat cleric, Bishop Morton, chose to stand in the shadows, watching them all. His coal-black eyes seemed like bits of stone, absorbing what little light there was in the tent and returning none of the warmth.

Richard had disliked Morton on sight years ago and time had not changed his opinion. The cleric had emerged as a friend to the Queen and her relatives, the reviled Woodvilles. If that wasn't enough to condemn him, Morton treated those beneath him as if they were dirt between his toes, while to curry favour with Edward, he smiled his slippery smile and lowered his eyelids to hide the light of his ambition.

Richard tried not to let his disgust show on his face. No doubt, like a serpent changing its skin, opportunistic Morton had chosen the path of the church not because he believed in God's word, but because it led the way to power for a man with ability but no means. Probably the same applied to his accommodation with Edward after Tewkesbury. He had set aside his Lancastrian sympathies not because he had transferred his loyalties to York, but because reconciliation meant he did not suffer the deprivations of exile. He had wormed his way into Edward's confidence with his considerable talents, but his greed and the devious bent of his mind condemned him.

"Not only did Charles not join forces with us in Calais," raged Edward, "but he bid us come to him in Peronne, and then he wouldn't let us within the walls! I swear he must be mad, for he knows not his own mind. And that turncoat St. Pol, who offered to deliver St. Quentin to us, instead fires on us when we approach! Now here we are, with Louis on the other side of the Somme."

Aye, here they were indeed, waiting for God knows what, using up precious reserves while Meg's husband, Charles the Rash as he had so aptly had come to be called, attacked Neuss. They could not wait much longer. Louis had laid waste the countryside and soon they would run out of food.

"We can win, Edward, even without Charles," Richard offered.

"What then? Without Burgundy we can't secure our backs! We're almost out of money and supplies, and we may not recover from such a victory." He marched to and fro at a frenzied pace, then halted abruptly. He turned to Hastings, eyes alight. "Have we captured any French nobles, Will?"

"Aye, Sire. One."

Edward strode over, hung an arm around Hastings's neck. "Hint to him that we may want peace... and let him escape to Louis."

From the shadows came a gasp of awe. "Ingenious, my Liege," smiled Morton.

Richard leapt to his feet. "*Peace!* We've not come all this way for peace." He threw Morton a look of contempt. Even the way the man spoke was devious. His lips didn't move, yet one heard the words clearly. "Peace would be dishonourable."

Edward's mouth twisted. "Brother, brilliant as you are, sometimes you confound me. You see about as far as a hooded falcon. Honour has no place here. We're talking about survival."

"What's survival without honour?" demanded Richard. "Once before you raised money for war with France and spent it elsewhere. The people have long muttered that you've deceived them! How will this sit with them?"

"However my subjects feel, I am their King, and the King sees no profit in war with France at this time."

"I'll have no part of such a peace."

Edward gave him a long measured look, his blue eyes cool, appraising. "'Tis the first time you've opposed me, Dickon."

"I won't compromise my principles, even for you."

"Mark my words, Dickon, your principles will be the death of you! Life is not black and white, but a mixture of greys. The sooner you learn that, the better for you." He strode back to the table, looking around at his councillors, who avoided his eyes. "How many are with Gloucester?"

Lord Howard finally broke the silence. Howard was one of Edward's most loyal and respected lords, whom Richard in childhood had affectionately nicknamed "The Friendly Lion."

"Sire, perhaps a dishonourable peace is worse than a useless victory..." Howard's voice faded and lost conviction as Edward's eyes narrowed.

"Honour be damned! You're out-voted, Howard. How to turn a bad situation to our favour, that's the question. If Louis is amenable to peace, we shall demand many remunerative conditions, one of which will be seven years of free trade."

"The people of England didn't give you their money for the chance to trade with France!" Richard shot back. "It was to recover the provinces of France which mad Henry lost."

"God's curse, brother, but you can be naive!" Edward slammed his fist down on the table, his patience at an end. "Nay, worse. Reckless. A damned fool. Fortunate for you that you're not king—you know naught of statecraft. Those territories cannot be won except with much money and even more blood. Is it not enough to humble France, enrich the royal purse so we never have to ask parliament for money again, return sons to their mother's with limbs intact, and save England from the burdens of a partial conquest in France? Is that not enough, brother?"

"It's not what you promised the people!"

"I promised them a victory over France. If I can get one without a fight, I shall take it, and gladly!"

"How can you trust Louis—a man who imprisoned a cardinal in an iron cage?"

"It would be good, for once, my brother, if you would see the facts without a moral squint."

"Louis can't be trusted! His money's a snare. If you take it, he'll own you. He'll trick you with his promises and destroy you, as he did Warwick!" Richard was shouting loudly. He knew all about Louis! Louis had wed Anne to Edouard. Louis's stink was still in his nostrils.

He fell silent, suddenly aware of the eyes on him; eyes that told him more about himself than he had ever suspected. Aye, he was against this peace because it was dishonourable, but that was only part of it. He hated Louis. He wanted to fight Louis because Louis had wed Anne to Edouard.

"I'm not Warwick!" Edward roared, red in the face. "I am *King*. No one owns the King!" He drew himself up to his full height. "I have made my decision."

Chapter 4

"Rain, rain, and sun! A rainbow in the sky!"

At the end of September Richard returned to a hero's welcome in England. All the way from the Cinq Ports north to Middleham, people lined the roads, flinging flowers in his path. They had heard how he had been the only one of Edward's councillors to refuse the French king's gold; how he had called it a bribe to his face. Richard rode along, nodding to the cheering crowds, his thoughts straying back to France. Louis's eyes had narrowed like those of a fox during their private dinner at Amiens when Richard had refused his bribe and cut the evening short. From henceforth he knew he would be marked as an enemy of France. That sat well enough with him. He would not parley with the man who had wed Anne to Edouard of Lancaster. Nor would he compromise his honour. As Edward had.

He compressed his mouth. Not only had Louis agreed to pay Edward an exorbitant annual sum, but he had betrothed his son and heir, the Dauphin, to Edward's daughter, seven-year-old Elizabeth. Since Richard had resolutely opposed the treaty, he didn't attend the signing, choosing instead to watch from his tent on the river bank as the two kings met. And a strange sight it made; one he would never forget.

The ceremony had taken place near the village of Picquigny on a special bridge that had been hastily erected over the River Somme. Edward, majestic in a black velvet cap gleaming with a jewelled fleur-de-lis and a gown of cloth of gold lined with red satin, strode across to meet Louis midway. The King of France, who cared nothing for the trappings of power, wore a grey coat, a shabby black hat, brown hose, and old black boots. He was followed by a dog. Edward had called the French King a gnat, but Richard thought that Louis embodied his nickname: *Spider. A menacing black spider clever enough to brighten his web with the gold that had lured in a splendid fly.* From the distance Richard thought he saw Louis gazing at Edward with the rapture of a spider permitting a fly to buzz helplessly, knowing his doom lay close at hand.

Edward's voice had held an eerie note as it floated to Richard over the water. *"Peace to this meeting and to our brother France!"* Then came Louis's voice, nasal, heavily accented, and somehow ominous. *"Most worthy brother England!"* They sat down on either side of a wooden barrier and conversed. A splinter of the True Cross was brought. Edward and Louis each knelt and kissed it, swearing to uphold the treaty. With a flourish of the plumed pen, they signed. Motioning their attendants away, they sat and conversed amiably with one another for several minutes. Richard had heard his brother roar with laughter and saw him embrace the French king in farewell. He remembered that a flock of geese swam past, quacking loudly, and at that moment a crane dove for a fish, caught its prey, and flew off. An omen?

On the following day Charles of Burgundy stormed into Edward's tent. A short, podgy, arrogant man with a bad temper, Charles had accused Edward of jealousy and double-dealing. "Jealousy?" Edward had inquired with raised eyebrows. "Aye, for I am descended from John of Gaunt and my claim to the English crown is better than yours!" declared Charles. "When I've finished with Neuss, I shall invade England and the people will rise up to place me on the throne, for they hate you and love me!" With that, he had stormed off. Edward had thrown his head back and roared with laughter. "Warwick was right about one thing—Charles *is* mad."

Richard grinned, remembering. Then his grin faded. His poor sister Meg; this was her husband.

No, the treaty did not bode well for England now that Louis owned Edward. Only one benefit had come of the miserable pact. Whether over guilt at the treaty he had made, or to pacify his angry brother, no one knew, but Edward finally granted Richard's old request that he had long refused. He gave the last of the three Neville brothers, Archbishop Neville, his freedom.

Richard had taken the good news to the Archbishop at Guisnes. He was shocked at his condition. More gaunt and frail than ever before, his tall frame bent by illness, George Neville was a broken man.

"I would invite you to sit," said Anne's uncle, attempting a smile and indicating the torn, lumpy mound of straw on the floor that could scarcely be called a mattress, "but the pallet has lice."

A vision of a rosy-cheeked George Neville jauntily striding along the halls of Middleham Castle at Warwick's banquet flashed into Richard's mind. That was before Edward's detested Queen had come between them. He, Richard, had been ten years old then, and the King and Kingmaker had been friends and allies.

"I deplore the conditions under which you have been imprisoned, my good cousin. I tried to ameliorate them, but to no avail. The Woodville Queen..." Richard broke off. Such talk was dangerous and normally he didn't make mistakes. The terrible shock of seeing John's brother this way had made him forget his usual prudence.

"My Lord, I know I have you to thank for my freedom now. I am grateful not to die here..." A dry, hoarse cough racked his thin body and sent him gasping for breath.

When the fit finally subsided, Richard said, "The York climate may prove too harsh for your health. I shall request you be returned to your duties at Westminster, my gracious cousin, if that is agreeable to you." He turned his reluctant gaze on the bony face. George Neville fell to his knees and pressed Richard's hand to his lips. "May you be rewarded for your Christian charity, my Lord Richard!" he sobbed. Gently, Richard had raised the feeble old man to his feet.

As he approached the walls of York, Richard forced the memories away and concentrated on his surroundings. Crimson and gold adorned the trees this fine September morning, and the sunlight was so bright it made his eyes ache. Children came running to view the procession, laughing, their hounds at their heels. Men left their ploughs to wave and cheer. Maidens appeared, curtseying, smiling, flinging flowers from aprons full of wildflowers.

Soon he would be home in Middleham with Anne and Ned. Home... Far from France, and far from court.

Chapter 5

"Fair and dear cousin, you that had most cause
To fear me, fear no longer. I am changed."

At Middleham Anne stood at the foot of the grand staircase of the Keep, awaiting Richard's arrival as a duchess should, quiet and dignified. But at the first blow of Gloucester Herald's horn, she was unable to restrain herself. She grabbed Ned from Nurse Idley, ran through the arched stone gateway, over the drawbridge, and down the hilly path, hair flying, the babe in her arms. Richard flung himself from his saddle and, amidst the smiles of his retinue, swept them to him.

Later, Anne listened as Richard vented his anger at King Louis, at the treaty, and at Edward's councillors, nodding her head in agreement; but in her heart she was glad there had been no war. For the first time in her life, a softness crept into her thoughts of Edward. Honour was all very well, but as Edward himself had pointed out, he'd returned men to their families alive, with limbs intact. Was that not enough?

The following month of October passed happily. They celebrated Richard's twenty-third birthday and watched eighteen-month-old Ned take his first sure steps. All Hallow's Eve was a special treat. Ned was now old enough to delight in the bonfires and revelry, and his pleasure only heightened theirs, but on All Saint's Day they had to kiss him goodbye. Much as Richard and Anne hated the court that swarmed with intrigue and Woodvilles, they were leaving for Westminster. Her mother by marriage, Marguerite d'Anjou, the once-fearsome French Queen of Henry VI, had been ransomed by Louis and would soon leave England. Anne wished to bid her farewell.

Even the sun loathes to shine on London, Anne thought as her palfrey stepped daintily through London's streets. Not only were the streets gloomy, but narrow. Narrow streets that ran between narrow houses and reduced the sky to narrow strips. London suffocated her. They passed the Mews where the king's falcons were kept. The clock in the tower chimed the hour of six, and the dying sun cast a rosy glow over the white castellated walls and towers of Westminster. The gilded barges on the river glittered, but the beauty was fouled by the air, which was putrid with the odour of fish and horse droppings, and rife with shrill cries, shouted orders, whirling wheels, and horses' hoofs. Anne cringed. She had barely arrived and already she craved the freshness of the moors and the solitude of the North. And her babe—how she missed him! She also wished Ned could have come with them, but he was delicate and they dared not take him far from Middleham.

Ned is curling up in nurse's arms about now, she thought wistfully, *to be sung a lullaby before bed.* She glanced at Richard riding solemnly beside her. He'd been against this trip. He said she owed Marguerite nothing, not even a farewell. He was wrong. Marguerite had once been kin. And there was another reason why she had to come, one she couldn't admit to Richard. Though her first husband, Edouard, had hated her at first, and though he'd always pretended it in front of his mother, he had shown her kindness at the end. It was Edouard who had consoled her in her grief after Barnet and the death of her father and beloved uncle John. Holding her gently as she wept, he had dried her tears and sworn to protect her. Sometimes in the dark of night she heard his voice: *Fear not, fair wife, for I have come to love you. If Lancaster triumphs, you shall be my queen, and I shall be proud for it.* Bidding Marguerite farewell might not mend anything, but it was a gesture Anne felt compelled to make. For Edouard's sake.

The November morning blew in with rain and wind.

"Are you certain you wish to do this, my dearest?" asked Richard as they stood together on the windy wall-walk that led to the Wakefield Tower—the same tower where Henry VI had been murdered on Edward's orders. "It's not too late to turn back."

Anne shook her head.

Reluctantly, Richard let her go. He watched as she approached the entrance of the privy chamber where Marguerite waited for Louis's envoy to take her to back to France that afternoon. He wondered if Marguerite knew that her husband had died in that very room, and if she did, whether she also knew that Edward had purposely lodged her there as final revenge for her murder of their father. He saw Anne reach the iron-hinged door and pause, as if she was reconsidering. He almost called out to draw her back, but restrained himself. This was her choice. He hoped it was not a mistake to let her go.

As Anne walked stiffly toward the door where Marguerite d'Anjou waited, six years slid away and she was a girl in a borrowed blue satin gown whose heart was breaking with hopelessness and despair. Behind that closed door waited a woman in black velvet and a prince with a contemptuous smile. She saw the girl and the prince in the Cathedral of Angers. Hand in hand they knelt, the girl and the prince, while the Bishop of Bayeux concluded the Wedding Mass, spread his bejewelled hands and said, *"Benedicite..."*

A man-at-arms thrust open the door.

Anne stared at the silent figure before her. The dark hair was grey now; the head once held so proudly high drooped on her chest. Hollow and drained, Marguerite d'Anjou sat in a simple wood chair. Just so had she sat in Cerne Abbey.

Anne approached.

Just so had Marguerite sat as Sir William Stanley strode into the nave with long steps, the heels of his boots clicking loudly on the cold stone floor. He had not knelt, but stood as he gave Marguerite the news of her son's death, a smile on his lips. Anne had taken in his gloating expression but she had not shared in his triumph. There was only sadness in her for Edouard, dead at seventeen, and for all the lives that had been sacrificed, and something akin to pity for the old woman in the chair at Cerne Abbey.

For old she had become, Marguerite. Bent and stooped and frail, all in the flash of a moment. Anne had reminded herself that this woman she pitied was the same one who had hated her, abased her, who had driven her father to his death and might have taken her life had the outcome of Tewkesbury been different, whatever Edouard had promised. For in Marguerite hatred had been a vital life force, surging and pounding in her veins and bursting forth in fury against the world when it could no longer be contained. Marguerite had hated her as she'd hated all her enemies: with all the seething vehemence of her soul. Yet, try as Anne might, she could not return Marguerite's hatred. Hatred demanded energy, something she didn't have. Was she a fool? An anomaly? She'd never had the passions others had, never wanted what others wanted. All she'd ever wanted was love. All they'd wanted was power. Why was she so different? And what difference did it make in the end? For the one who'd wanted power and the one who'd wanted love both found themselves together in a cold abbey, their lives shattered, in a world forever changed.

Anne shook herself out of the past and gazed at the woman who sat before her in the simple wood chair. Aye, those had been her thoughts then, but the truth had eluded her at sixteen. *The path we choose does make a difference.* Poor Marguerite. She had found hate, and hate had found her. Anne forced the memories away and quickened her pace towards the woman in the chair. On the table near Marguerite a document lay open, the black ink still wet. She angled her head and read:

> I, Marguerite, formerly in England married, renounce all...
> to Edward, now King of England.

A small, battered wood coffer stood in the corner. All Marguerite's possessions, in one small coffer. As a girl of fifteen, she had come to England with nothing, and now, thirty years later, she was leaving with nothing. Her father, Rene of Anjou, had sold his kingdom to Louis to raise the fifty thousand crowns for her ransom. In France, Marguerite would have nothing either. Anne knelt and put her arm gently around the former Queen. "You are free now, Marguerite," she whispered softly. "You shall go home." Marguerite's head fell against her shoulder and all Anne could think of as she cradled the old grey head was how strange life could be; how unpredictable, and how cruel. Then Marguerite lifted her head and turned her dead eyes upon her. "You have a son," she said.

Anne smiled, "Aye."

"So had I once," Marguerite replied.

Anne rose, shivering with sudden cold, and fled the chamber.

Richard never learned what passed between Marguerite and Anne, for Anne never told him. All he knew was that the meeting had been disastrous. When Anne had left Marguerite, she was trembling uncontrollably. Convinced that some ill had befallen Ned, she had clutched him fiercely and refused to let him go until he promised to send to Middleham for news. That night she had come down with fever. For a week at the Palace of Westminster she lay in bed, plagued by her old childhood nightmares—terrible imaginings about gargoyles and broken glass. Richard knew he'd been right. No good ever came from visiting the past.

Chapter 6

"...black, with black banner, and a long black horn."

C hristmas of 1475 was a happy one at Middleham, even though the New Year blew in with a fierce blizzard burying the north in snow. Oblivious to the howling winds that strained against their windows, Richard and Anne frolicked with their little Ned, secure in their joy.

Richard was relieved that his presence had not been required at court in months. His life in Middleham had acquired a regularity that agreed with his character. He had never liked change; had always found it threatening. For too long change had meant death, distress, upheaval. In the familiar daily routine that marked his life in these days, there was security and comfort, for he knew what to expect, as with a well-beloved melody. He devoted himself to his family, his estates, the Marches, and to the administration of justice for the people of the North, and felt himself complete as husband, father, son-in-law, and overlord.

As spring worked its magic over the land, he took Anne to York on his council business. Then, in early June, came a festive event that brought the entire Gloucester household to the city of York: the pageant of Corpus Christi. The only disappointment was that Anne's uncle could not attend. His health was too delicate for the journey, Archbishop Neville wrote from London, promising to come before long.

A lavender and rose dawn streaked the sky as wagons gathered on Toft Green and began their descent, winding through the streets and pausing to enact biblical scenes along the way. Shipwrights, fishmongers, and mariners performed the tales of Noah; goldsmiths, the three kings from the east; and vintners, the miracles at Cana. It was a great spectacle, involving at least fifty guilds and many hundreds of performers. Ned loved it, clapping his hands and shrieking with delight.

Exhausted but happy, Richard and Anne returned to Middleham

the following afternoon. They were greeted with the news that a messenger had arrived early that morning from London and awaited with urgent tidings. They hurried into the great hall. "My Lord," said the messenger, a monk, "the Lord Archbishop Neville is dying." Anne and her mother embraced tearfully.

Archbishop Neville did come again, as he had promised, but not as anyone would have wished. He came to be interred in the crypt at Yorkminster.

Middleham soon healed the grief of his passing, for at Middleham there was little Ned to spread laughter through the castle. But three months later, only a week after Richard's twenty-fourth birthday, while he was away at York attending a meeting of the Council of the North, a messenger arrived from Northumberland. Anne was on her knees, singing to Ned in the nursery, when her mother came in, her face etched with sorrow. Anne ceased her song. She handed Ned to Nurse Idley and rose. "John's Isobel is dying," said the Countess. "We must go to her." Anne felt the sting of tears.

Anne and the Countess reached Bisham before Isobel's second husband, William Norris, had returned from the south, where he had journeyed on business. In the abbey where Nevilles had been buried for centuries, where John lay with his father Salisbury, and his brothers Warwick and Thomas, and where Isobel had come to be with John, they found her drifting in and out of consciousness. The physician informed Anne and the Countess that she had caught a fever soon after the birth of her dead child. At thirty-five she was not yet old, the physician said, and certainly she was strong enough to recover, but she seemed to have lost the will to live.

With her chestnut hair splashed across the pillow, Isobel seemed strangely young and innocent, and Anne had been moved to deepest pity as she gazed on the still-lovely face. Isobel had asked Anne to take her ten-year-old son, George, to be raised as a Neville, which Anne readily agreed to do; but her last words had made no sense. They were directed to John, whom Isobel thought was standing at the door. Isobel had given a little laugh and said to the door, "I keep telling you, my Lord, angels have golden hair, not chestnut... Oh my love, I come..." and the brilliant smile that illuminated her face froze on her lips.

They had wept, the Countess and Anne. Later, as they rode home, Anne pondered Isobel's last words. "Might she have seen uncle John?" Anne asked her mother, who knew much of death. The Countess shook her head. "Such dying visions, though not uncommon, are merely imaginings brought on by fever." Anne found herself disappointed. She wanted to believe that John had truly returned for his precious Isobel.

More ill tidings followed on the heels of Isobel's death, unleashing a load of sorrows almost too great to bear. On Christmas day, in the midst of revelry, soon after John's young son, eleven-year-old George Neville, came to live with them, a black-clad messenger arrived from Warwick Castle, where Anne's sister, Bella, lived with her husband, Richard's brother, George. The minstrels hushed their song. The Countess rose to her feet unsteadily, ashen pale, trembling. Anne reached for her mother's hand.

He bowed stiffly. "Your Grace... my Lady... I am the bearer of grievous tidings. Her Grace, Isabelle, Duchess of Clarence, died three days ago giving birth to a son."

The Countess swooned. She was carried out of the hall, followed by a sobbing Anne and a sombre Richard. That very day a black pennant went up over the castle and the greenery that decorated the windows was covered with mourning cloth. As church bells tolled ceaselessly telling of death, Richard and his little family kept prayerful vigil at the chapel.

Soon another missive arrived. The babe, too, had died, passing from this world on Christmas day. Grief ushered in the New Year of 1477.

At Warwick Castle, fury exploded in George, Duke of Clarence, with the thunderous violence of a tempest at sea. His entire body trembling, he poured himself another goblet of malmsey and slammed down the emptied flask. *Damn you, Edward. The Fiend take your foul soul!* He downed a gulp of the strong, sweet wine and wiped his mouth with his sleeve. All his life his elder brother

Edward had lorded it over him, telling him what to do, where to go, what to think! All his life his vile brother had pushed him around, laughed at him, and belittled his accomplishments. He wouldn't take it anymore!

He grabbed the empty flask and flung it against the wall. His accursed, stinking brother had forgotten that he owed his throne to him! But for his defection from Warwick at Barnet, Edward would never have won the battle. Now, to return the favour, to secure him a crown, all the ungrateful knave had to do to was grant him permission to ask for Mary of Burgundy's hand. And that he had refused.

Refused!

Reaching for a full flask, George knocked his goblet down, splashing red wine over the table. He put the flask to his mouth and gulped, spilling more than he swallowed. How dare Edward deny *him*—a prince of the blood royal—and put forward Anthony, that low-born churl, brother to the Woodville whore whom Edward called his Queen! He hurled the empty flask at a man-servant quivering in the corner of the chamber. "Wine!" he roared, rage boiling his blood. "Can't you see it's empty, you stupid bastard?" *Bastard*. That's what Edward was! He called himself King but the truth remained: Edward was a bastard, the son of an archer. He had no damn right to the throne. He, George, was rightful King of England.

The man-servant scrambled back with the pain-killing Spanish wine George loved. He upended the new flask and drank greedily. That was why Edward hated him, why he had humiliated him before all the world, why he kept trying to poison him! The only reason he was still alive was because he was too clever for Edward. When he went to court, he took his own cook and brought his own food.

He slammed the flask on the table and dropped his head into his hands. *Poor Bella*. She hadn't fared as well. If only she had listened to him! Instead, she'd trusted that midwife sent by the Woodville witch while he was away, a mistake that cost her life. A searing anguish tore his gut and he laid his face flat on the table in the cold wine. Sobs swelled in his throat and convulsed his body.

Bella had died, and soon afterward, his infant son had joined her. Murdered by Edward and his sorceress Queen!

He sat up abruptly, eyes blazing. *God's Blood, they weren't going to get away with it.* He'd make them pay—the midwife who'd tended Bella and the doctor who'd poisoned his newborn son! He pushed himself to his feet. Swaying unsteadily, he crashed a fist down on the table. "Summon my captains!" he roared. "We're going to hang those murderers Twynho and Thuresby! By God and all His saints in Heaven, those whoresons are going to pay!"

Once he'd dealt with them, he'd take care of Edward, the accursed lying bastard who called himself their father's son.

About to enter the great hall at Barnard's Castle, Richard stood unnoticed for a moment, watching Anne rock Ned in her arms as she sat framed by the oriel window that had been his wedding gift to her. Four deaths, all in the span of six short months. Archbishop Neville, George's newborn babe, and the two Isobels—both dead within two months of one another. He had brought his little family here for the spring, hoping the change would do them good, and later, had taken them to York for the festival of Corpus Christ in June. At his suggestion, he and Anne became members of the Guild to honour Archbishop Neville's memory. It had been a glorious summer's day. The city of York had sparkled, for the streets had been hung with arras and the doorways strewn with rushes and flowers. In a dazzle of torches, tapers, crosses, and banners, they had walked in the procession from Holy Trinity Priory to Yorkminster, surrounded by smiling guild members, clerics, and officials of York who bore the gem-studded shrine of silver gilt that contained the sacred elements.

For a short while it had helped to be among laughter, but they had returned yesterday, and already Anne was listless, the Countess was weeping in her room, and young George Neville, so recently orphaned, was left alone without comfort to mourn his own loss. *If only George had not cut Bella off from her mother and Anne... If only George had permitted Bella to visit them, it might have gone easier on them all,* Richard thought. The Countess had not seen her daughter since their days of exile in France before the Battle of Barnet, and she'd never met Bella's two children, one-year-old Edward and three-year-old Margaret. Her grief was wretched. All because of George.

God, how hateful George had been!

Richard braced himself and crossed the chamber. Anne was still unaware of him as she cooed to Ned, explaining the lay of the land. Aye, even in the rain, the view was splendid. Mist bathed the treetops and the river glistened like crushed crystals. The sound of gushing water was so comforting he could almost forget what he had to tell Anne. He stood mutely a moment, seeking words for the news he bore.

Heaving a heavy sigh, he looked down at her. "Dearest, I must go to London on a matter of great urgency."

Anne turned abruptly from the window. Her eyes flew to him in alarm and, though her lips parted to speak, no words came.

Richard bit his lip. They had everything now. *Peace. Love. Ned.* Yet fear had come to join them, a shadowy, unmistakable presence hovering beneath the surface. He had prayed fervently for an end to the ill tidings, but the new year had arrived on a note of death and gloom, which it seemed would continue. In January, Meg's husband, Charles, that half-mad duke of Burgundy, was killed besieging another inconsequential town. He left no male heir, only a daughter, Mary, so King Louis declared that Burgundy had reverted to the crown of France. Meg appealed to Edward for help, and Edward vacillated. Though England's trade was at risk, he had no desire to lose the fifty-thousand crowns Louis paid him yearly. And his Queen, ambitious Bess Woodville, desperate that Edward not jeopardise the marriage which would one day make her mother of the Queen of France, also agitated against Burgundy.

Richard had journeyed to court briefly in February to attend Edward's council meeting and argue in support of Burgundy. There he found aligned against him faces he had hoped not to see again for a very long time: the murderer, St. Leger, now brother-by-marriage to him; that devious man of the cloth, Bishop Morton, whom he had always despised; the Queen's brother, Anthony Woodville; her son Dorset; Edward's debauched companion Hastings—and cold, hard Henry Percy, a former Lancastrian for whom Edward had inexplicably sacrificed their faithful cousin, John Neville. These here had urged Edward not to move against France, but to wait and see what developed. His muscles tensed beneath his topaz doublet. *Of course they had.* Like Edward, they didn't want to lose their pensions from Louis. Unfortunately, what developed was not much to Edward's liking.

In view of Edward's reluctance to support Burgundy, Meg offered another proposal: that George, a widower since Bella's death, wed her stepdaughter, Mary. The marriage would keep Burgundy in the English orbit, Meg said, and George could at last wear a fine coronet if not a crown. Edward rejected Meg's proposal and refused George permission to ask for Mary's hand. His reasoning was clear: George was trouble enough at home under his watchful eye. He had no desire to put into his hands power that would surely be used against him.

As far as Anne was aware, that was where the matter ended. But there was more. Richard had kept it from her.

Ned had fallen asleep in Anne's arms clutching the velvet blanket she had embroidered for him. He was a sweet babe, good-natured, with a sunny disposition. He loved to laugh and romp, and showed a lively curiosity about his world. In all ways save one, he was everything they could wish for. *If only he enjoyed better health!* Richard bent down and adjusted his coverlet. He was always battling some rash, or illness, or chill, and twice this winter he had burned with a raging fever that lasted a full month, causing them much worry. He'd be glad when Ned was grown and the troubles of childhood were behind him.

Richard watched Anne disengage Ned's little fingers from around the gold cross that hung at her neck and hold him out to his nurse. He rested his hand on Anne's shoulder and their eyes followed Mistress Idley and her charge until she disappeared from sight into the stairwell of the Keep.

Anne patted the silk cushion. "Come and sit, Richard." He settled beside her on the window seat. "Now tell me why you must go to London."

"'Tis to do with George."

"Let me guess. He's asked Mary of Burgundy for her hand despite

Edward's refusal to allow him to do so?"

"Nay, it would have done him no good if he had. As it turns out, Mary herself was against the match and wouldn't have accepted George. She said that what she needs is a great prince who can defend her dominion against Louis, not an English duke who will bring her nothing but trouble."

"George must be furious."

"Aye, he's convinced Mary would have married him had Edward granted permission to bring his suit. And Edward..." Richard hesitated, drew a deep breath, "...spitefully crowned George's injury with an insult. He gave the Queen's brother, Anthony Woodville, permission to ask for Mary's hand."

"Mary is the richest heiress in Europe; the Woodvilles are low-born! Has Edward gone mad?" The moment the words fell from her lips, Anne wished she could recall them. This was no time to start a bitter argument. She braced herself for Richard's response, but it was not what she expected.

"Edward's not altogether in his right mind. Bess Woodville has cast him under her evil spell." He fell silent and a faraway look came in his eyes as he gazed at the river.

So he is beginning to see the faults in Edward, Anne thought. Yet the old loyalty demanded the blame be placed elsewhere.

Lost in thought, Richard stared at the river, seeing Warwick's face in the rippling currents, hearing his voice in its roaring. So much of what Warwick had foretold had come to pass. Charles of Burgundy had proven as mad and useless an ally as Warwick had predicted, and had practically served up Burgundy to Louis on a silver trencher, just as Warwick had warned. If Meg had married into France, how much better would it have been for her—and for England...

Warwick had been far too accurate about another marriage as well. The Woodvilles had proven the plague he'd feared. He recalled the prophecy Warwick had made to Edward: that his Queen was a woman so reviled throughout the land, no son of her blood would ever be permitted to mount the throne of England. A dread prophecy, for kings were not ousted without war. *If only Edward hadn't married that woman!*

But, unable to help himself, Edward had wed Bess Woodville in a secret marriage after a chance meeting in the woods where she had lain in wait for him during a hunt. Months later, he'd made the marriage public and unleashed her on the land. She was the cause of his rupture with his Neville cousins, and the cause of civil war. The image of the council chamber at Reading Abbey where Edward had announced his secret marriage flared in his mind. Once again he saw John's ashen face, saw Warwick pounding his fist on the table.

And so began the rift that led to civil war. Richard shook the memories away.

"My dearest, there's more... Two months ago, in April, George sent his men to abduct Bella's midwife, a woman by the name of Ankarette Twynyho, from her home in Somerset. They brought her to Warwick Castle where George charged her with poisoning Bella."

"Tell me she didn't do it, that it's not so!"

"Nay, my little bird, it's all in George's sick and clouded mind. Ankarette Twynyho had been sent to Bella by the Queen. No doubt she was a talebearer, but the woman would never stoop to the foul murder of a duchess. She protested her innocence to the end and George had to force the justices to condemn her. She was dragged off to the gallows, along with a doctor whom George claimed had poisoned his babe."

"Why would George do such a brutal thing?"

"By taking the King's justice into his own hands, he wants to show the land that he is rightful King... He once put out the story that Edward was the bastard son of an archer..." Richard rose abruptly from the window seat, the old doubts about his own paternity assailing him once again. As far back as he could remember, he'd been tormented by the thought that he was no true Plantagenet. The evidence had seemed overwhelming to him as a child: in a family of blonds, he was dark; where they were self-confident, he struggled to find his place in the world. His brothers were tall, powerfully-built natural warriors, while he had been born puny and of average height. Only by study and force of will had he overcome his handicaps. Even now as a grown man the dragon of his childhood nightmares appeared at times of strain to cry out that he was a bastard.

He had always doubted himself, but only George could doubt Edward.

"A shameful tale for it impugns our mother's honour. Now he's sent his servants through the land to proclaim that Edward practises the Black Arts and has ordered his followers to be ready in armour within an hour's warning. It seems he'll stop at nothing to gain the throne."

"God help us!"

"Anne, there is more…I would keep all this from you if I could, my dear one, but I may be gone a long while and the tales that come to your ears may be more fearsome than the truth."

Anne jerked back her head and looked at him wide-eyed.

"There has been a prophecy…" Richard hesitated. "…that the King will be succeeded by one whose name begins with the letter G."

George. Anne held her breath.

"The prophecy has unsettled Edward. One of George's servants was executed three days ago for trying to procure the King's death by sorcery."

"He was innocent, too," Anne whispered. "The Woodvilles."

"Aye, the Woodvilles drove Edward to it… They've been plotting George's downfall for a long time, and with George's own help they're succeeding."

She closed her eyes on a breath. Why wouldn't the past stay buried? Like an ugly tune that ended and returned to the beginning to start over, the past kept repeating itself. "You had a messenger today," she said, her voice a bare whisper. Last year they had returned from the joyful Corpus Christi celebrations in York to a waiting messenger and the news that her uncle was dying. Yesterday they had attended those same ceremonies. In the outpouring of love and merriment around her, she'd managed to forget her sorrows for a few hours, but from the moment she'd espied the Sun in Splendour emblem of the royal messenger, she had felt unsettled. She'd persuaded herself that it was only fatigue. After all, they had celebrated for two full days and walked through the streets for hours. Now she had to face the truth. That emblem had always meant trouble. For her father, and for Richard.

Richard nodded grimly. "That's when I realised I could no longer keep all this from you. The messenger bore evil tidings, Anne." His jaw clenched. When he spoke again, his voice was thick, unsteady. "George has been charged with treason and taken to the Tower."

Chapter 7

"O brother… woe is me!"

Richard's pleas to Edward to pardon George were singularly unsuccessful. Though his mother journeyed from her castle at Berkhampsted to add her voice to his, Edward remained curiously impervious to their entreaties. Richard was unable to comprehend his intransigence. Edward yielded neither to logic nor brotherly love, not even to their mother's anger and condemnation. As he strode with Edward through the cloisters of Westminster Abbey on an overcast September morning before he departed for Middleham, Richard pressed his brother one last time. An unseasonably cold wind blew their cloaks about their legs and the silent arches threw long dark shadows across the stone walk. Richard shivered from the cold, but as much from the unease that held him in its grip.

"You've always pardoned George's treasons; what is different this time?"

"The prophecy," said Edward. "That 'G' will rule after me. It will not happen, by God!"

"Once there was another prophecy. It said your sons would never rule and your daughter Elizabeth would be Queen in their stead. Have you forgotten? That also troubled you. They cannot both be true."

"Nevertheless, I am decided."

"God's curse, Edward!" Richard blurted, halting in his steps. "What has come over you? Have you gone mad? We're talking about our *brother.*"

"A brother who's spent his life wronging us. Why do you persist in your pleas? Of us both, you have more cause to hate him than even I."

"Whatever his sins, he's our brother. You can't live with his blood on your hands. I beseech you, for the love you bear me, forgive him." He looked up desperately into Edward's resistant face. A muscle quivered at Edward's jaw and his mouth was clamped so tightly shut, it resembled a blade. The strain of the past months had taken a harsh toll. Richard thought of a lyre and a string pulled so taut that it would surely break. He drew a sharp inward breath. "Something is different this time… 'Tis not the prophecy that impels you, is it?"

Silence.

A gust of wind shrieked along the cloister, tore at their mantles, and was gone. All was still again except for the cawing of ravens. Richard stood transfixed, unable to drag his gaze from Edward's face. It was as if Edward were aging before his eyes, as if the mask that hid the true set of his features was now melting away. He was shrinking, his face growing more pinched and haggard as, line by line, pain etched itself deeper into the creases around his eyes, the grooves around his mouth.

"It must be done!" Edward cried out suddenly, his voice quivering in a way that Richard had never heard before. He pressed his hand to his brow, and dropped it, exposing eyes filled with agony. "I have no choice."

A sudden, terrible realisation struck Richard. He stared at Edward in speechless horror, his mind reeling. *It is not the prophecy that compels Edward. It is Bess Woodville.* This foul deed had her seal on it. She had found a way to force Edward to kill his own brother! He clenched his fists against the revulsion that flooded his body.

Richard returned to Middleham in a despondent mood. The respite proved brief. Soon he and Anne had to return to Westminster to attend the Christmas festivities, which were to be crowned by a royal wedding. Finding himself strangely in need of a connection with his dead cousin, John, he borrowed Thomas Gower away from young George Neville for the journey. John's faithful squire was now squire to John's son, and not only had he rendered long and faithful service to the Nevilles, but he was a solid man, inherently dependable and, at forty-six, the same age John would have been, had he lived. With his carved features, kindly eyes, and reserved temperament, Richard found in him a comforting sense of John's own presence.

Spirits were high at the Woodville court. Gaiety was everywhere. With Edward, though, Richard knew it was forced, because he'd glimpsed his soul that day in the cloisters and knew that what Edward did, he did in spite of himself—not that the knowledge made it easier to bear. With a gloom and foreboding unmatched since the days of civil war, Richard ushered in the New Year of 1478 at Windsor, his hand clasped tightly in Anne's.

Anne shared Richard's mood. Not only did court bring back wrenching memories, but the Queen and her ilk kept looking at her and whispering. She had overheard one of Bess's sister's remark: "How has she survived such storms when she looks as if the next breeze will carry her off?"

"Do not fool yourself," Bess Woodville had replied. "The tiny red finch, barely a spark of life and weighing scarcely more than a feather, is not swept away by the merciless winds of winter."

Then they had laughed.

No, there was nothing redeeming about court, not a moment she enjoyed. Her head throbbed most of the time and sleep was fitful. It didn't help that she worried about Richard, whose misery struck at her heart. A heavy burden of guilt weighed on his spirits for participating in a celebration that gave the Woodvilles cause to rejoice when his own brother lay confined to the dark of the Tower.

Early on the morning of the wedding day, Richard escaped the Woodvilles and slipped out to St. Stephen's Chapel. The January morning was bitter cold and a rare drift of snow swept the cloisters. In the side chapel of Our Lady of the Pew, he stood alone, admiring the lofty, narrow nave, the great columns gilded by thousands of leaves of gold and silver foil. Sunlight played on the cold, brilliantly coloured glass, sending darts of cobalt blues, violets, oranges, and yellows through the gloom. The peace which had eluded him since his arrival at court found him now. He knelt and murmured a prayer for George.

No sooner had he risen than a door clanged and footsteps sounded on the stone. His cousin Henry Stafford, Duke of Buckingham, strode up jauntily. "We must have had the same idea, Dickon—to get away from Woodvilles for a spell!" With a twinkle in his eyes, Harry chuckled, "'Tis the only place not infested with them, eh? Not enough gold around, I suppose…" He surveyed the nave festooned with pine branches and greenery. Richard almost smiled in spite of himself.

"Yet even this dull church has its uses. Behold the holy Woodville altar!" Harry jerked his head in its direction. "Another heir, another sacrifice. Nevertheless, the child is blessed, isn't she? She's too young to understand the ill turn her life has taken. Ah, well, so it goes…" He sauntered off, his gem-encrusted hat and claret doublet flashing like a beacon in the subdued light of the nave.

Richard watched with soft eyes. He liked his cousin. Their mothers were sisters, but the dukes of Buckingham had been Lancastrians and had fought for Marguerite d'Anjou. After Ludlow, when Richard and his mother became prisoners of Harry's father, he and his little cousin had played many a ball game together. Richard had always been struck by the resemblance between his cousin Harry and his brother George. Both were the same age; both had the same golden curls, the same easy charm and love of fine clothes, and the same loathing of Woodvilles. The young Duke of Buckingham, one of the richest and most noble heirs in the land, had been snatched up by the low-born Queen at the age of eleven and married off to her sister, Catherine, against his will. Harry had never forgiven Bess Woodville for that. Richard understood his enmity.

The wedding service was finally over and the four-year-old prince, Richard of York, Richard's own namesake, was wed to the greatest heiress in the land, six-year-old Anne Mowbray, daughter of the dead Duke of Norfolk. Richard's sole pleasure in the ceremony was an act of charity he performed at his own request. Dipping into a basin of gold coins, he scattered them among the crowds gathered at the chapel doors. Then he dutifully escorted the child-bride into the Painted Chamber for her wedding banquet.

Fragrant ambergris scented the air and the floor was strewn with dried rose petals and violets as Richard led Anne Mowbray to the head table and lifted her into her chair beside her husband. A handsome child, little Richard had been scrubbed until he gleamed and he looked very fine in his white silk hose, gold shoes, and white cloth of gold doublet sewn with pearls and diamonds. His nephew was only a year older than his own Ned and he bore Richard's name, yet Richard felt no affinity with the child. His milk-white complexion and pale hair stamped him too clearly as a Woodville. With a stiff bow, he withdrew to take his own place at the end of the table, beside Anne.

She gave him a faint smile and pressed his hand as he sat down. He could use comfort. The hall glittered with candles and torches, and in their light the rich coloured wall murals glimmered much as they had years ago when the Irish Earl of Desmond had made his fatal visit to England. At that banquet, the charming earl had attracted the enmity of the Queen, and soon afterwards, he and his two little boys, mere babes at six and eight years old, were sent to the block. Well did Richard remember that night. The same unease gripped him now.

He watched the festivities with glazed eyes, his thoughts on George a short distance upriver, alone in the Tower. He upended his cup, drained the fine Gascon wine in a single draught, and held the cup out to a servant for refill. He stabbed a slice of roasted boar with his dagger, brought it to his mouth, then set it back on the golden trencher. He couldn't eat; his stomach was clenched tight. He glanced around the room wretchedly.

It was a merry group that feasted and revelled in the flowing wine as servants brought hundreds of silver platters of venison, peacock, and swan to their banquet tables. The din of their conversation and raucous laughter resounded through the hall. He noted with bitterness that Bess Woodville herself was in high form that night. Her smile was expansive; her jewels larger and more plentiful than ever before. Louis's fifty-thousand crowns were clearly in evidence. Ever since the Treaty of Picquigny, Edward's court had grown lavish. Behind Bess Woodville and all around the hall, chests of silver- and gold-plate glittered coldly in the torchlight. Richard remembered a comment he'd overheard Bess make to Edward years earlier: "A country's wealth is in its plate, is it not?"

"Aye," Edward had replied, eyeing her with affectionate amusement.

"And the more plate, the more respect. So we must always display our plate in plenty."

She must have displayed the entire treasury, Richard thought dryly.

Bugles announced the dessert course. There was blancmanger, jellies, plum pudding, and a grand marchpane subtlety. Carried in by four knights, it was in the form of a massive throne with the back and the armrests embossed with fleur-de-lis. Eight-year-old Princess Elizabeth was lifted up into it and seemed a tiny feather in the chair as she was carried about the hall to cheers and applause. Afterwards a knight carved the French throne into edible portions with his sword and servers bore them to the guests.

Richard's mouth curled with distaste. He doubted the marriage would ever happen, though Edward still believed Louis to be a man of his word.

A troubadour arrived to sing of a knight who courts a shepherd girl. The jewelled guests dissolved into laughter at the ridiculous twists of the tale, but Richard was lost in his own thoughts. Next came a dancing bear. He watched her antics and turned to gaze at Edward, who was roaring with laughter. *It wouldn't be so easy for Edward to leap across the table to dance with the bear now as he did at Middleham years ago,* Richard thought. Edward had grown fat. His richly embroidered flowing robe of blue satin with its ample fur-lined sleeves hid his bulk well, but nothing could hide his bloated face. Along his nose ran a fine web of tiny red and purple veins, and beneath his puffy eyelids his eyes were like arrow-slits. Layers of sagging fat buried the once elegant cheekbones and strong jaw that had given definition to his good looks. As for his complexion, he had traded the bronze that comes with too much sun for the florid hue that comes with too much wine. Richard's gaze passed from his brother to the woman sitting next to him. The woman responsible.

Bess Woodville no longer smiled. Cold and haughty, she sat with her back rigid, her passionless green eyes watching everything, missing nothing. Her famous beauty, which Richard had never appreciated, had dulled with age and prolific childbearing. Since 1466 she had given birth every two years, providing Edward with five daughters and two sons. The Woodvilles were breeders, that much had to be said for them.

His eyes moved to her brother, Anthony Woodville, sitting beside the Queen. He was pontificating on a new book that was the talk of the court. *The Dictes and Sayings of the Philosphers* was newly published by William Caxton's printing press, which Caxton had set up at the sign of the Red Pale, an edifice in a court of almshouses next to Westminster Abbey. Anthony Woodville had translated the book into English and Caxton had dedicated it to him. "'Tis a French manuscript which came into my hands on my pilgrimage to St. James of Compostella," he was saying to the old Duchess of Norfolk, a smug expression on his face.

Richard pressed his lips tightly together. When Caxton came to England, he'd sought George's patronage, but thanks to the Woodvilles, George was in the Tower. Now the book, which should have been dedicated to him, was dedicated to a Woodville. Richard picked up his dagger. What had Warwick called them? *An infestation of beetles rotting the ship of state*, or some-such. He had been right. Voraciously they ate and multiplied, these omnivorous, all-devouring greedy beetles, destroying everything in their path. They respected no one and nothing—not even the laws of the land. The Queen, driven by her insatiable greed, had forced the dowager Duchess of Norfolk to surrender her property to her little daughter, Anne Mowbray. Then, subverting all laws of inheritance, she had seen to it that her son was given absolute title to the Norfolk estates, even in the event of his little wife's death. Not content with that, she had persuaded Edward to take back the dukedom of Bedford from George Neville, John's son.

Richard's hand clenched around his dagger. He had been with Edward here in this very room when Edward had informed him of his intention. "John loved you!" Richard had reminded him, stunned. "Were it not for him letting us pass at Pontefract, you would never have regained the throne!"

"Were it not for his treason, I would never have lost it!" Edward had shot back. More calmly, he'd added, "Besides, Bess wants the title for little Dickon."

Aye, Edward has changed, Richard thought; no longer was he the generous, undaunted, sunny-hearted prince determined to see justice done. She had changed him with her witchcraft and greed for gold. "Money, money, money," Edward had once laughed to Bess. "You do love money, don't you, my sweet?"

"No more than you, my Lord," Bess had replied. And Edward had laughed again, and given her a lusty kiss, not seeing the difference between them. They both loved money, aye, but Edward wouldn't kill for it.

Nevertheless, Edward, driven either by guilt over his infidelity or by love for Bess—Richard couldn't decide which—was unable to resist her evil acts. She had plunged the realm into civil war and made England bleed torrents of blood. She had cut Edward off from one brother and now threatened the life of the other. She had destroyed everyone whom she deemed a foe, even innocent babes. And Edward hadn't resisted her evil acts. Those evil acts had brought him down to what he had become. They had tainted what greatness he had achieved. They would destroy him yet. Richard stabbed at the table with his dagger. *How he hated Woodvilles!* The blade caught in the wood and quivered.

Bess Woodville turned her haughty head. For a long moment their gaze locked and held. He met her eyes without flinching until she finally looked away. He felt a momentary satisfaction. Only George had ever dared to challenge her that way.

"Dickon, you're not eating." It was Edward. "You're not laughing. Surely there's something that pleases you?"

"No, Edward. Not while our brother languishes in the Tower."

Edward's expression stilled. "He has brought it on himself," he muttered.

Richard reached across the table and grabbed his sleeve. "Let him go, Edward!"

The musicians broke into a bright melody with their pipes and tabors and drums. Edward snatched his arm away. "I've told you before, I could not even if I would." He pushed back his chair and offered his hand to Bess. She took it and rose. Richard watched as Edward danced with his Queen, and thought it fitting that neither of them smiled.

Chapter 8

"O purblind race of miserable men…"

On the day after Prince Richard's wedding, as Abbey bells rang for Tierce, Parliament convened in the Painted Chamber. Edward seated himself on his canopied throne while Richard and his royal cousin Harry, Duke of Buckingham, disposed themselves on a lower step of the dais.

"My lords," Edward began, glancing around the room that only the night before had been full of merriment, "I have assembled you here today to try my royal brother, George Plantagenet, Duke of Clarence, on an attainder of high treason."

Silence.

"Very well, then," said Edward, pushing out of his gilt and velvet throne with a rustle of his black robes. "I shall begin by listing the charges against the Duke of Clarence." And list them he did. The repeated treacheries. His own repeated pardons.

When he was done, George answered him. "I am rightful King of England! For you are not our father's son! You are the bastard son of an archer and have no claim to the English throne!"

Gasps of horror were drowned out by Edward's roaring voice. "You foul liar. You mad idiot. How dare you sully our mother's honour for your own ends."

"This is but one of the charges I levy against you!" cried George, red-faced, eyes bulging. "There are many others…" He listed his right to the throne by blood and by the act of King Henry's parliament. He revisited the long list of perceived wrongs done him by Edward, culminating in the murder of his wife, Bella, and the murder of his newborn babe.

Edward cursed. George cursed back. For an hour the arguments flew.

"Enough!" Edward finally slammed a clenched fist on the gilded armrest of his throne. "I have heard enough. Your verdict, my lords!"

Fear was palpable, and for a moment no one spoke. Then someone murmured, "Guilty," and the dull murmur of *Guilty* ran through the chamber. In the silence that followed, the gentle patter of the falling rain rose to a deafening pitch. Edward averted his face and sagged against his throne, gripping a pommel tightly. He raised a feeble hand in dismissal. The guards approached George.

"Let us settle this once and for all, Edward," George called out suddenly. Edward jerked his head up at the first civil words George had uttered all morning.

"If you will make due submission, George," he said, descending from the dais, "even now... all will be forgiven."

Eyes blazing with hatred, George threw his jewelled gauntlet at Edward's feet. "I make no submission! I challenge you to mortal combat and the judgement of God!"

A sharp intake of breath resounded around the chamber. Edward's face tightened with anger. "Fool!"

"Bastard!"

Edward swung on his heel and stormed out of the room. On trembling legs, barely able to breathe, Richard followed.

Prince Richard's marriage festivities continued for another week. A joust was held at Westminster and the chief challenger was Anthony Woodville. Clad in white brocade and ermine, and riding a black horse caparisoned with black velvet and white silk, he was the most splendid figure of the day. Richard did not attend.

On the seventh day of February, a special meeting was convened in a stone-vaulted council chamber at Westminster. Harry, Duke of Buckingham, was appointed High Steward in Richard's place, to spare Richard the painful duty that would have otherwise fallen to him.

George was brought in. Buckingham rose stiffly. "You are adjudged guilty of treason," he read. "By the laws of England and by order of His Grace, King Edward IV, you are hereby sentenced to death."

Richard's breath caught in his lungs. He shut his eyes and sagged against the wall.

It was snowing when Richard's mother, Cecily, Duchess of York, arrived at Westminster in a last effort to save her son George. Tall and regal, wearing the black she had worn since her husband's death eighteen years earlier, she cut an imposing figure. For ten days she pleaded, threatened, and negotiated with Edward for George's life, with no result except that she stayed Edward's hand. Then the Speaker of the Commons came to the bar of the Lords and requested that whatever was to be done be done quickly.

Richard was with Edward in the great hall when Buckingham delivered the Speaker's request. Visibly shaken, Edward gave a curt nod. Buckingham bowed hastily and retreated to join a party of lords sipping wine in a corner of the chamber. Richard followed Edward to the window. Resting his full weight on his outspread hands, Edward searched the Thames as if those icy waters held the answers he sought. A short distance away, on the dais beneath a tapestry, the Queen sat playing dice with her five daughters. Her mind was clearly not on the game, for her glance kept stealing to them.

She's like a vulture drawn by the scent of carrion, Richard thought, clenching his jaw. His gaze returned to Edward, who had lifted his head and now seemed to be staring at the royal figure of Richard II in the embrasure of the window. Deposed by the Lancastrian Henry of Bolingbroke, it was Richard II's murder that had ruptured the rightful succession and set into motion the events that ended in the Wars of the Roses. Above a gilded canopy a blue angel with outstretched wings held out a crown over the dead king's head. Aye, for that crown much blood had been spilt—blood which had drenched the soil of England red. For that crown had poor saintly Henry been murdered. For that crown George would die.

Richard said, "Edward, you refused my pleas for Henry's life. Now your immortal soul is stained with his blood. God may forgive your regicide, but the murder of a brother—'tis too much to ask, even of God, Edward."

"I refused your pleas for Henry's life," Edward said, without turning. "Now we've had six years of peace in the realm. I refuse your pleas for George's life and we shall have peace again. Peace, peace…" He thrust the windows open and frigid air struck them both in the face. Richard shivered, but Edward stood silently as the wind whipped his hair and stirred his furs, staring fixedly at the river.

"Remember Cain and Abel," said Richard, breathing hard. The final moment had come. There would be no other chance. "Remember your vow to our father."

Edward turned and Richard was startled by how ghastly he looked. In the harsh blue light of day he was ashen pale and his bloodshot eyes were encircled with deep shadows. A muscle twitched in his left eyelid. Richard knew it was a sign of strain.

"I did vow to look after you both," Edward said in a drained voice, "and I have, Dickon… I've done my best, but it's not been enough, not with George…" His mouth worked with emotion. "I have no wish to do this any more than you would in my place, Dickon… If only I didn't have to."

"Edward, give him a last chance. Henry had it. Surely it's not too much for your own brother?"

The silence that ensued seemed endless.

"I'll go to him in the Tower tonight," Edward replied.

Richard laid a hand on his sleeve in gratitude. "Together, pray God, we'll talk sense into him."

"I go in alone."

Richard stared, seized by unease. Only one reason could there be for such a strange condition between brothers. Edward had something to hide.

The February night was cold and a few frosty stars glittered in the black sky. Richard waited in the torchlight at the foot of the outer staircase and watched as a man-at-arms admitted Edward into George's chamber. The same room had once been Henry's, and Henry had died there. A cold shiver ran down his spine. Fixing his eyes on a star, he gathered his confused thoughts and focused his mind on prayer. He didn't know how much time had elapsed, but the loud clang of a door startled him.

Any hope he'd nursed of a reprieve dissolved with the sound of angry footsteps thudding down the stairs. He watched Edward approach, and looked up miserably into his face. "He deserves what's coming to him!" Edward hissed, and strode off with his torchbearer, leaving behind only the click of their boots on the cobbles as they faded into the darkness.

That very night George was executed in the Tower. Richard never learned how George died, but soon afterwards a story began to circulate that he had contemptuously requested death by drowning in a vat of the sweet malmsey he had loved so much. With the exception of the lands of Richmond, which he'd once given up to placate his jealous brother, Richard refused the lands and titles that Edward offered him from George's estates. He did, however, accept the earldom of Salisbury for little Ned. It was an honour that had belonged to Anne's Neville grandfather and meant much to her. But Richard's other request, that George's little son, Edward, and his daughter, Margaret, come to live with him and Anne at Middleham, was denied. They were heirs, and the vultures were circling. The orphans became wards of Dorset.

For two tortured days Richard was unable to eat or sleep. He sat silently with his lute, looking out at the river, strumming the melodies that George had loved as a boy. But nothing relieved the terrible pain.

"Richard," said Anne late one night, "you cannot go on like this. Come, try to sleep, I beg you."

Richard looked at her with stricken eyes. "I hated George," he said, his voice cracking. "I wished him dead. I can't live with the guilt, Anne…"

She sat down beside him. She could not share his distress over the death of her old persecutor, but time, distance, and contentment had long since allowed forgiveness to replace the hatred in her heart. And well did she understand loss. She took his hand gently into her own. "Then you must appease your guilt, Richard. You can't help George anymore in this world, but you can help him in the next."

The following morning Richard sought Edward in his royal bedchamber. He found him alone, lounging in a chair by the fire, toying with a wine cup, emptied leather flasks rolling about at his feet. On a nearby table the stacks of papers that awaited his signature remained untouched. "Edward," he said, "I wish a licence to found two religious foundations, one at Middleham and one at

Barnard's Castle."

Edward lifted his wine cup and downed it with a trembling hand. "The purpose of these colleges?" he asked, avoiding his eyes.

"To house priests and choristers to pray for you and the Queen, and for friends and kin who died in battle…" He hesitated, looked at Edward, "and for all those of royal blood, living, and dead."

Edward rose heavily, dropped his hands on Richard's shoulders. "Good brother," he said with moist eyes, "your licence is granted."

Chapter 9

"All is past, the sin is sinn'd, and I,
Lo, I forgive thee."

St. John's Day, 1480, was a happy one at Middleham. The castle gates and windows were flung wide to the summer sunshine and the feast was celebrated on the grassy slopes outside the castle walls amid laughter and song. Ladies strolled, children made merry, dogs barked, and young men picked wildflowers for their lady loves. Richard and Anne lounged on a crimson blanket, watching Ned frolic with the hounds while servants passed back and forth with food and drink, minstrels played, and men kicked balls and gambled at dice.

"How happy everyone is, Richard!" Anne said, rolling to her side and propping her chin on her hand to gaze at him. "I grew up here, yet in all my life I've not seen Middleham this way. In my father's time our windows were shut, our gates barred against attack, for we were Yorkists in Lancastrian territory..." Her glance roamed over him lovingly. Dressed in his favourite dove grey, which complimented his dark hair and bronzed complexion, Richard's eyes were clear as melted pewter in the sunlight. A smile played on his generous mouth, softening the clean lines of his jaw. "You've done this, Richard, my love."

"Nay," said Richard. "All I did was to get the city of York exempted from Edward's taxes. 'Tis for that they love me, Flower-eyes."

She laughed. He stretched out lazily and looked up at the sky.

Anne hugged her knees and smiled. How sweet it was to see her husband so content and little Ned play with such delight. And to hear Richard call her Flower-eyes. What a glorious day it was! A strong breeze blew, rustling leaves and bearing the scent of pine and the bleating of sheep from pastures below the village, and so many butterflies danced on the summer air it seemed wildflowers had taken wing. She wished there were more days like this for Richard. Thorough and painstaking in all he undertook, he rarely indulged himself as he did now. A curious thought struck her. He seemed to be drinking deep from the cup of pleasure as if he knew it would be empty for a long time. Was it because he had just returned from the Scots border? Or was it because he was bracing himself for the morrow?

"I wish you didn't have to go to London, Richard," she said, a trifle anxiously.

"I won't stay long. You know 'tis only to see Meg that I go at all." With a smile, he reached out and patted her hand. "Let's not think on that now, my little bird. It only spoils the joy of the hour."

She nodded, and he closed his eyes. But the bitter taste of court lingered in her mind. As Edward had predicted, peace had come to England with George's death. *Peace—at least for Edward,* she thought. The Scots continued to give trouble, but it did not disturb him one whit. That heavy mantle fell on her husband's shoulders, just as it had once fallen on her uncle's, and while Richard kept peace in the North, Edward returned by day to his affairs of state, and by night to his sybaritic pleasures. It was rumoured he had a new mistress, a certain Jane Shore who had won his heart and was very beautiful and kind.

How different might it all have been had good-hearted Jane Shore come along fifteen years ago! But it was Bess who wore the crown, and now she craved another in France. As a result, Edward had never sent his sister Meg the help she needed to keep Burgundy safe from Louis of France. Mary of Burgundy had married Maximillian of Austria after George's death, but not even that great prince could hold out against Louis alone. He'd sent many emissaries to Edward with pleas for help, but Edward continued to vacillate, to the detriment of England's trade and the hardship of the people of both Burgundy and England.

And so, driven by desperation, Meg was coming to press her brother herself. She'd have no better fortune. Edward would choose wine over war, whatever the cost. With Louis's fifty thousand crowns a year and George's income of three thousand, he had grown complacent. There was even money enough to build a magnificent chapel at Windsor, a true masterpiece of architecture, which Edward had dedicated to St. George. In his brother's memory, she presumed, to appease God for his fratricide. Aye, it would take a magnificent chapel to do that...

Anne pushed her sour thoughts away and tickled Richard's nose with a wildflower. He smiled, caught her hand, and looked at her steadily with his deep grey eyes in a way that made her heart pound.

"I wish I could make love to you right here," he said under his breath. "If only we were alone."

"And that, my Lord, we certainly are not!" she laughed, taking a candied rose petal from one servant and a cup of sweet wine from another. She sipped daintily, her glance moving over the crowd. Small groups stood around mummers and men on stilts, laughing and munching, and children romped together, giggling. A knight strolled through the crowd with a pretty lady on his arm, and they paused to watch a monkey entertaining a group of noble ladies. Closer by, in the shade of a mulberry tree, her mother sat in a carved chair, stroking old Percival's ears, a contented smile on her lips as young George Neville read to her from Sir Thomas Malory's manuscript on the tales of King Arthur's court. Anne wondered if John's son knew that what he read had, in part, been drawn from Malory's own life experience during the Wars of the Roses between York and Lancaster. First a Lancastrian, later a Yorkist adherent of her father, Warwick, Malory had run afoul of Edward's Woodville Queen and had been imprisoned without trial for ten years. During this time he wrote Morte d'Arthur. Richard had obtained his release after Warwick's death at Barnet, but Malory, old and frail, had died soon afterwards.

To Anne, the similarities between Malory's portrait of the damsel who besotted Merlin and Bess Woodville were undeniable, but no one had ever dared mention the resemblance. To do so would be a foolhardy act of suicide. Edward's vengeful and detested Queen had shown her power when she annihilated the House of Neville, the mightiest barons in the land. Now the Woodvilles ruled supreme in the realm, the power behind Edward's throne.

John's son was fifteen now, a fine-looking lad with tawny hair and topaz eyes. *But what marvel in that, when John and Isobel were his parents?* She blinked to banish the sudden ache that came to her at the memory of her beloved aunt and uncle, and turned her attention to Ned, throwing twigs for the hounds to retrieve. *Beloved Ned,* she thought. He always chased away the sorrow and brought a smile to her lips.

Richard followed her gaze. Ned was five years old now, a small mirror of themselves. His dark hair stamped him firmly as his own son, but in the vivid blue of his eyes, the shyness of his smile, and the flash of his dimples he could find John, Warwick, and Anne— all whom he loved. No doubt the resemblance to Anne's father and uncle bound the child even more tightly to Anne's own heart, for she fussed and fretted over Ned constantly and her eyes never left him. Sometimes she even sat by his cot as he slept, staring fixedly. *Watching him breathe,* he thought with a smile. Yesterday he had seen her strolling along the ridge of the hill with Ned following and old Percival dragging up the rear. They had been etched in sharp relief against the vivid blue sky, and a thought had come to him with an ache. She seemed like a duck with only one duckling. But God be thanked that they had Ned. It didn't have to be so.

He leaned back on his elbows and raised his face to the sky. Wispy clouds drifted across the blueness and flocks of blackbirds winged overhead, their distant cries mingling with Ned's laughter to make sweet music in his ears. He fastened his attention on that music so his mind might not stray to what he must tell Anne before the day was out.

Beside him Anne felt the effects of sunshine and wine. She gave her empty cup to a passing servant and stretched out on the crimson blanket, savouring the muted sounds and fragrant scents borne by the wind. Soon her lids grew heavy and she closed her eyes.

Ned's sudden shriek pierced the air. Richard and Anne both bolted upright at the same moment.

"Lady Mother, Lord Father, see, I have a sword!" Ned cried out, dragging a large twig. "A big sword!"

Relief flooded them and their hearts began to beat again. "And big it is, that branch; longer than you are tall, my Ned," said Richard, still recovering from the shock. "But you are a strong boy and can manage it, can't you?"

Ned nodded proudly.

"My Lord Earl!" announced a voice sharply. Ned swung around. It was Richard's bosom friend Francis Lovell standing legs wide, arms folded across his chest. "My Lord Earl, I challenge you to a duel!" Francis flung his gauntlet at Ned's feet, his lips twitching as he strained to keep a grave face.

"I accept!" Ned said with great excitement. He picked up the gauntlet, handed it decorously to his father and, using both hands, lifted his pretend sword. Francis lumbered forward on his club foot and grabbed a twig. They began a careful dance forward and back, taking turns lunging at one another. "Surrender, my Lord!" cried Ned, tiring. "I am the best knight in the land and you are no match for me!"

"Indeed," replied Francis, lunging to miss. "And who are you?"

"Sir Percival," shouted Ned. At the sound of his name, old Percival rose from beside the Countess's side, trotted slowly over to Ned and Francis on his arthritic legs and, exhausted by the effort, collapsed between them with a heavy sigh. Francis turned to grin at Richard. At that moment Ned poked him in the groin with his branch. Francis coloured and lifted one eyebrow in surprise.

"A mortal wound, my Lord Earl…" he exclaimed while Richard and Anne chortled. "I am undone—undone—aaah!" He fell to the ground as if dead.

"Well done, fair son!" cheered Richard.

"You crossed branches most elegantly, my lords!" Anne cried, throwing a shower of daisies over them.

Ned laughed and ran off to chase a hound, and Francis sank beside them on the long grass. "Nothing like a child to make us play the fool, eh Francis?" Richard grinned. Just in time, he caught himself from adding, *Time you had one of your own.* Francis had long been ready for children. The trouble was that his wife, Anne Fitzhugh, refused him her bed. She had never forgiven Francis his club foot and the years had hardened her into a cold and carping woman any man would wish to shun. Richard thought how fortunate he had been, not to have met the same fate.

A woman with red hair strolled by with her knight, laughing.

For Richard, it felt as if someone had slapped him in the face with a gauntlet. That red hair, that laughter, stabbed at his breast, leaving him awash in guilt. He had no more heart for merriment; he forgot the sweetness of the day. There was only Kate, as she had looked the previous week at Pontefract. Poor Kate. God forgive him, he had not known how much he had hurt her. Though he visited his two bastard children whenever he was in Pontefract, by mutual agreement they had not seen one another since that day in September '71 before his marriage. Then came Kate's summons. He had gone to her with deep unease, and it had turned out even more painful than he had feared.

He stole a glance at Anne, conversing with Francis. Before the night was over, she would have to know about Kate. Partly from his own cowardice, and partly because he knew how it would wound her, he had put off telling her until time had run out and left him no alternative. He gnawed his lip and toyed absently with the gold griffin ring John had given him. His head throbbed and his stomach clenched into a knot. He felt hot and dizzy. He'd had too much time to think today, that was the trouble. Suddenly leisure seemed an intolerable burden and he rose abruptly, desperate for something—anything—that would keep his mind off the task that lay ahead. Francis and Anne stared up at him in surprise. "I'm going for a hunt. Care to join me, Francis?"

Francis scrambled to his feet. "Why not?"

Anne's smile was forced. She had sensed a sudden strange disquiet in Richard. As she watched the friends walk off together, her heart no longer felt so light. Richard had never cared for the hunt.

Anne did not move. She stood at the window, staring down at the dark garden as if carved of stone. At a loss, Richard didn't know what else to do, what to say. He had expected tears, accusations, anger, but not this. This stillness. He had never seen her like this before. They'd had their little spats now and again, mostly about his family, but she had never withdrawn from him this way.

"Anne… I was only seventeen… I believed you lost to me forever… That was the only reason, I swear it! I never loved her—never pretended to…" He moved to take her shoulders, and dropped his hands helplessly. There was no forgiveness in her. It was as if an invisible shield separated them.

All Anne could think of as she stared into the dark night was that she was barren, her only babe sickly, and this woman had borne Richard healthy children, one each year. By now there would have been a full bevy. Healthy, laughing children. This other woman had triumphed where she had failed. And she hated her for it.

"Anne, they're innocent, Johnnie and Katherine... They didn't ask to be born; they have a right to be loved. There's no one else to take them... Kate..." He almost choked on her name, knowing how much pain it had to cause Anne. "Kate's going into a nunnery; the children have no one but me... Us..." He stood awkwardly, waiting for something, anything. There was no response. "Christ, Anne, Johnnie's named for your own uncle of Montagu! Does that not make a difference?"

Silence.

Richard closed his eyes, utterly bereft. She had every right to be angry with him, but it was the children who would pay: sweet, loving eight-year-old Katherine, and lively, even-tempered Johnnie. Kate had done well with them. He felt the nauseous sinking of despair and pressed his hand over his face. He'd hoped to give them a good home at Middleham, and that Anne might come to love them as he did. He had wished Ned to know his brother and sister so he wouldn't grow up alone. Now they would have to be sent away—Katherine into a convent to be raised and educated, and Johnnie into an abbey. They would be cared for well enough; that was comfort. Their physical needs would be met, and they would learn about God and history, Latin and Greek.

And loneliness.

How he wished he could spare them that! But it was inevitable, unless Anne could find it in her heart to give them a chance...

Her rigid back told him it was useless. He supposed he should leave, but he felt drained, too exhausted to move. "I shall be gone before the cock's crow," he said in a weary voice. "You needn't see me off." He dragged himself to the door, rested his hand on the iron latch. He hesitated, turned back. "I was nine, Johnnie's age, when I came to Middleham fatherless. You loved me then. It changed my life..."

He floundered, awash in misery and guilt, pulled the handle, and strode out the door.

Anne brooded the night. *I've never been good enough. Richard never loved me; not really.* Another woman had claimed his heart the moment she was gone. Visions of their naked bodies danced out of the darkness, taunting her, slicing and wounding without mercy. She saw the woman smile at him, heard him whisper her name. *Kate.* Their kisses grew more passionate; they entwined arms and legs and began to rock violently in frenzied lovemaking. The lurid details slashed at her, drawing blood as deeply as a whip on soft flesh. Hate and revulsion swept her and she trembled with a rage she had not known before. For the first time in her life she felt a deliberate desire to maim, to inflict punishment, to destroy. She slammed into Richard's bedroom.

"Be gone!" she yelled at the servants sleeping in the antechamber, giving one of them a kick. They ran out in terror. "And shut the door!"

Richard, seated in the window, leapt to his feet in astonishment, nearly dropping the lute he had been strumming softly by candlelight.

"How dare you!" Anne screamed. "You deceived me! Betrayed me! Lied to me! And now you expect me to raise your bastards as my own? How dare you!"

Richard paled. This wild-woman could not be his gentle Anne! Even her voice had changed from the soft tones he knew to a harsh guttural sound that emanated from another place deep within her throat. She was trembling uncontrollably, her uncombed hair fell over her shift in rats-tails, and her fists were clenched at her sides. He had thought anger was preferable to the silence with which she had met his confession, but this maelstrom was enough to put the fear of God into the King's own champion. "Anne…"

She strode up to him and slapped him hard across the face. Stunned, Richard wiped his mouth with his hand and stared at the blood her rings had drawn. His own temper flared. "All lords sire bastards!"

"Aye, when they marry for lands!" she fired back. "You swore you loved me, and you betrayed me!"

"I did love you; why can you not understand that—and forgive?"

"I'll never forgive! Never, ever. And you can take your bastards and drown them for all I care." She whirled around and stalked off. Richard was seized with a fury of his own. He ran after her, caught her arm and swung her around. "And what of you? Why should I not expect understanding when you deceived me and betrayed me, and took my forgiveness as your due?"

"You're mad! I never deceived you!"

"With Edouard of Lancaster? You bedded him, and willingly, didn't you? Didn't you?"

She backed away. Richard matched her step for step until he had her pinned against the wall, arms above her head. "Tell me about it, Anne! Were his kisses as hot as mine? And his manhood, how did that compare? Did you cry out for him like you do for me...?"

"Cease!" she screamed, twisting her face away from his. "I hate you. I hate you!"

"You hate me. Did you love him?" He tightened his grip of her wrist. "Speak! I want the truth!"

"Let me go..." She writhed to free herself. "You're hurting me!"

He slammed her hard against the wall. "Not until you give me the truth!"

She burst into tears. He dropped her wrist in confusion, retreating. "I'm sorry, Anne... I don't know what came over me... I never meant to hurt you; I swear it."

She looked up at him, silent tears rolling down her cheeks. "The truth is... we began by loathing each other..."

He held his breath. He had not realised how desperately he needed to know until this moment.

"...and he ended by loving me."

Richard swallowed. "And you?"

"I... I don't know what I felt—but it wasn't love."

"What then?" he whispered hoarsely, his heart pounding.

"More... like pity."

"Did you weep for him when he was dead?"

She didn't respond for a moment. Then she gave a nod. Richard closed his eyes.

"Not in the way you think," came the sweet voice he knew.

His eyes flew open.

"I wept because… because there was good in him… and he died brutally, betrayed by one he trusted…" She met his gaze. There was no need to add that it was Richard's brother George, Edouard's brother by marriage, who struck seventeen-year old Edouard down on the field as he begged for mercy.

"I regret that, Anne… I regret many things."

"So do I, Richard." She raised her hand to his cut cheek.

"That will heal." He kissed the palm of her hand.

"I don't know what came over me. It was as though a demon possessed me… I was jealous because I couldn't give you more children, and she did." Tears stung her eyes. She broke off, bit her lip.

"My love," he said gently, tilting her face up to his, "'tis a relief that you can give me no more children."

Her lashes flew up. She stared at him, violet eyes bewildered.

"I nearly lost you with Ned. I could never go through that again, my little bird." He bent his head and kissed the hands he clutched between his own. "Forgive my jealousy of Edouard."

"Oh, Richard," she said, gazing at his dark head. "We both did what we had to do. What else could we do?"

He gathered her to his breast and held her close. After a long moment she looked up at him. "I'll make arrangements for the children. They'll be here to greet you when you return."

"Thank you, Anne," he murmured into her hair. "Thank you, Flower-eyes…" He crushed her lips beneath his own.

Chapter 10

"I know, God knows, too much of palaces!"

Richard arrived at Windsor on the Feast of St. Swithin to find that Edward had spared no expense for the visit of their sister, Margaret, Duchess of Burgundy. In a grand gesture he had sent his fleet, headed by Bess's brother, Sir Edward Woodville, all the way to Calais to escort her to London. With minstrels playing and oars dancing in the sparkling waters, she was transferred to a royal barge festooned with flowers and streamers and brought up the Thames to Greenwich Palace. There, after a lavish pageant, banquet, and gift-giving ceremony, the glittering court gathered in a torch-lit chamber adjoining the great hall. Richard was conversing with his sister and a group of her ambassadors in a corner of the room when Bess Woodville drew up to Meg.

"Have you heard, fair sister, how matters go with Marguerite d'Anjou in Reculee? Is she content?"

"Content? I think not, Madame. In truth, she is no longer in Reculee but in Dampierre, living almost in poverty. Louis—as you may be aware—is not an overly generous man." Meg's lips curled with distaste. Louis was notoriously mean with his gold. "Sometimes he fails to send her even the meagre pittance he agreed to. Yet she continues to provide for some old Lancastrians who are in dire need and have nowhere else to go."

Bess gave a measured sigh. "Thankfully, I cannot reproach myself. I was good to her and did what I could to ease her lot while she was here, in spite of the expense. She was a queen, after all." Hoping no one remembered that she herself had been Marguerite's lady-in-waiting before marriage to Edward elevated her to Queen, Bess rushed on. "I remember one particularly generous gift of mine, a black velvet gown with miniver at the collar and cuffs, which cost the royal sum of fifty marks..." Bess had kept careful tally of the expenses she had incurred for her former benefactor, and of them all, this was the one she most regretted. "I do believe the services of my physician, Dr. Lewis, also meant much to her. Indeed, how is her health?"

"Not well, Madame."

Bess raised her plucked brows carefully. "How so?"

Meg turned to one of her advisors, a tall, distinguished-looking gentleman with a heavy golden collar that announced him Treasurer of the Order of the Golden Fleece. "You have seen her, Monsieur Gros. What was it you told me? I have forgotten."

"I did not actually see her myself, Your Grace, but I haf spoken to one who has," he said in an accented guttural voice. "His report vas dat her eyes are hollow and dim, and perpetually inflamed—no doubt from constant veeping—and dat her skin is so dry and scaly, some think she may haf leprosy."

"Leprosy?" Bess gasped. "How revolting! Let us speak of more pleasant matters... Dear sister, how do you like my arras?" She gestured to the wall behind Meg with a fine white hand laden with enormous jewels. "'Tis the Siege of Jerusalem, wrought in pure gold. You have not remarked upon it, but I hope you find it worthy of us?"

Meg turned to look. So this was the famous arras for which Bess had ruined poor Thomas Cook, a rich burgher and former Mayor of London who had declined to sell his arras to her family for a paltry sum well below its worth. She herself had managed to get the old man, a good friend, released from prison the first time Bess had dragged him there, but Bess had him re-arrested as soon as Meg had left England to marry Charles the Rash. The tapestry had disappeared when Cook's house was ransacked by Bess's father. Clearly, Bess had stolen it and was not ashamed of her theft, even flaunting her prize openly. "Wonderfully pleasing," Meg managed, swallowing her disgust. Unable to say more, she transferred the burden to her Treasurer. "What think you, Monsieur Gros?"

Monsieur Gros took the hint. "Vonderfully pleasing, Your Grace, as you say." He turned to Bess. "However, might I add that the gold thread, though magnificent, has not the lustre of your gilt hair, Madame, and the royal maiden is but the shadow of your beauty."

Bess gave him a gratified smile. "So I am told."

A trumpet fanfare sounded. "Ah, the banquet begins."

Richard waited for Bess's long train of ermine and green cloth of gold to sweep past and witnessed Meg exchange a glance with Monsieur Gros that conveyed their thoughts more clearly than words: that Bess held her head higher than any queen of royal blood they had met on the Continent, and that there was a leprosy of the soul far worse than any of the skin. He offered his arm to his sister.

At Windsor later that evening, Richard strolled through the torch-lit gardens with Meg. It was a beautiful July night. A cool breeze stirred the trees and the sky glowed with stars, but he had no eye for the fragrant blooms or the hedges carefully manicured into animal shapes past which they ambled, and no ear for the laughter and song around him. Being at court with Woodvilles had brought back the anguish of George's death. Ever since George was executed, he had been plagued with dreams of his brother's death. He'd see himself in the Tower in George's place, his hands bound behind him, being pushed down steep, dark steps into a dank cellar where wine butts stood. He would be shoved face down on the cold floor and his knees strapped to his chest. Then powerful arms would hoist him up and throw him into the cold black liquid. As he struggled, the cover would be slammed down and secured. The darkness would be complete; the panic overwhelming. He always bolted upright from these dreams, drenched in sweat. Anne would light a candle and calm him.

Richard stole a sideways look at Meg, wondering how she felt about being here, among their brother's murderers. It could not be easy for her. She had loved George best, yet it did not show in her gracious demeanour.

She is growing old, he thought sadly. She was thirty-four now; six years older than himself. Tall and slender, she carried herself as erect as their mother, with as much dignity but none of the haughtiness. Though she hid the beautiful thick brown hair he remembered beneath a jewelled hat and veil in the severe style demanded by fashion, and though time had sharpened the angles of her face, which resembled their mother's more than any of his other sisters, yet she did not look hard. There was understanding in her blue eyes and a hint of a smile in the curve of her lips. He wished life had been kinder to her. She had known neither the love of a husband nor of a child, this sister who had given him a mother's love. Thankfully, she was not completely bereft. By all reports, she adored her stepdaughter, Mary, who was said to be very pretty and sweet-natured.

"And you, dear Dickon, are happy now at last," Meg smiled.

"Aye, Meg. Fortune has been kind to me in many ways."

"I have heard, my brother, how well you have done in the North. That wild Lancastrian stronghold is now reconciled to the House of York and devoted to you, so they tell me. It seems that justice is as much your passion, Dickon, as it was our noble father's."

"I've simply done what I believed was right."

"You are the only one of our brothers to take after him, you know."

Richard halted in his steps, looked at her. "I'm nothing like our lord father, Meg."

"That's where you're wrong. There is much about you that has always reminded me of him, God assoil his noble soul. Now I see that you have not only his face, but also his heart."

"But our father was fair, and I am dark," said Richard, struggling to suppress the doubts about his paternity that had plagued him since childhood.

Meg smiled. "Not as fair as you seem to remember."

Richard had been given that assurance once before, from a kindly Irish earl on a night almost exactly like this one. He hadn't believed Desmond, either. People saw what they wanted to see. Meg loved him, and Desmond had been a generous man. *Desmond, who was murdered by the Woodvilles.* A stabbing pain came and went. He gnawed his lip. A silence fell, broken by the gushing of the fountain they were approaching.

"Certainly you look well, Dickon," Meg continued. "'Tis more than I can say for Edward."

Loyalty kept Richard from voicing agreement with Meg's observation.

"The word on the Continent is that Edward has sunk into such lethargy he would bear any insult rather than fight," continued

Meg, undaunted by his silence. "That above all else, he is a man who loves his ease and pleasure. Louis jokes that he has had more success driving the English out of France than his father ever did, and his father had to fight, whereas the only weapons he used were venison patties and fine wines."

Richard heaved an audible sigh. "I advised Edward against the peace."

"I know. I heard. Louis thinks you are inflexible, unimaginative, humourless, and a warmonger."

"I care not what Louis thinks. I call my duty as I see it."

"You were the only one to refuse his gold."

"Sadly, that's true."

Meg heaved a sigh. "Terrible, terrible about George... I cannot understand how Edward could do it. Can you, Dickon?"

Richard lowered his voice and cast a glance over his shoulder before he spoke. "All which has come about, has come about because of the Woodvilles. Anne says George went mad after his first-born son died aboard ship. He blamed Edward and swore vengeance. George said it was Edward's fault for marrying Bess; that if Edward had done his royal duty and married for the sake of the realm, all would have been well."

"True enough. That infernal marriage tore the land in two. If only our father hadn't been killed, how different it might all have been."

"Have you ever wondered, my fair sister, if there is purpose to such turns of fortune?" ventured Richard. Doubts had come to him of late, since George's death.

Meg shot him a frowning look. "Ours is not to ask why, but to accept, my brother. All will be revealed in due course. Surely, you don't doubt that?"

"Of course not... not really."

"Good." After a moment, she added, "My son-in-law Maximillian cannot hold out against Louis, Dickon. He is young, vigorous, and a general of talent, but he has no money of his own, and his father, the German Emperor, can spare him no soldiers. Do you think Edward will give me the help I need, if I pay him the fifty thousand crowns that he gets from Louis?"

"War costs money, Meg. Even with your gold, he'd still be the loser. Besides, the Queen dreams of seeing her daughter, Princess Elizabeth, on the French throne. Ever since Picquigny, she's demanded the child be addressed as Madame le Dauphin, as if she were already married."

"Such pretension. 'Tis not for nothing the Woodvilles are despised. It is not their low birth as much as their low character." She fell silent a long moment, then gave a sigh. "If Edward puts his hopes in Louis, he shall pay dearly for them."

"Louis's gold has already caused England grief. Since Edward doesn't support Burgundy, trade suffers. Last winter was severe. Men's stomachs are empty. There's much restlessness, much disorder, throughout the land."

"Even in the North?"

"Even there, though not so much as elsewhere."

At that moment there was a shout. A ball flew past them and landed in the rose bushes at the edge of the pond. A young boy came tripping out of the hedges, his blue velvet doublet askew, his fair curls bouncing over one eye. "My Lord uncle of Gloucester, and my fair lady aunt, Duchess of Burgundy," he said with a proper bow, "have you perchance seen my ball?"

A slow smile twisted Meg's generous mouth. "I have, and perchance I shall tell you where it went, but first let me say how fine I find your manners, Prince Richard of England."

"Thank you, my gracious lady aunt, Duchess of Burgundy. My tutor makes me memorise two lines of Chaucer each time I forget my courtly manners."

"Aha, a wise and effective policy that will make a fine knight out of a very handsome boy," said Meg.

Seven-year-old Richard bowed again. "Thank you for the compliment, my lady duchess Aunt, but I must point out that I am not as handsome as I would like."

"Indeed?" exclaimed Meg feigning shock.

"One eye is lower than the other. If you look closely, you can see quite clearly." Pointing to the offending eye, he took a step forward and held his face up for her inspection.

Meg examined him. "Aye, I do believe you are right. 'Tis the mark of the Plantagenets that you carry, and a great honour. Your noble ancestors, Henry the Third and Edward the First, had it, and it absolutely does not detract from your good looks, my young prince. So if I were you, I'd forget all about it and chase my ball, which is right... there!" She pointed to the spot.

With another bow and appropriate ceremony, Prince Richard retrieved his ball and was gone.

"He is a dear child," said Meg.

"He is a Woodville," said Richard.

Chapter 11

"O golden hair, with which I used to play
Not knowing!
O imperial-moulded form, And beauty such as never woman wore,
Until it came a kingdom's curse with thee—"

Richard left for Middleham the same morning Meg departed England. In the ensuing weeks he devoted himself to his duties, but life did not resume its comfortable pattern. The Scots violated their truce again. This time they had crossed into Northumberland and burned Bamborough. It soon became clear that old Louis lurked behind the troubles. Anxious to keep Edward occupied while he took care of Burgundy, he had stirred up James of Scotland with his promises. In September Richard punished the Scots so soundly he ended their incursions, but by wet and blustery October, vexing problems with Henry Percy, Earl of Northumberland, replaced those with the Scots.

Many misunderstandings irked the touchy Earl of Northumberland. Though Richard tried hard to accommodate him, sometimes their conflicts couldn't be settled as amicably as he wished. Once they each backed different men for the post of Prior of Tynemouth and Richard's candidate won the position, to Percy's humiliation. At other times, when the city of York received conflicting commands, one from Percy, the other from Richard, they ignored Percy and did Richard's bidding—and Richard didn't always know, while Percy smouldered.

At length, by the exercise of delicate diplomacy, Richard managed to smooth Percy's hoary bristles long enough to gain his good will, and together they planned the campaign against the Scots that Edward had decided to wage come summer and which he would lead himself.

Lord Howard struck the first blow against the Scots in the early summer of '81. He won a brilliant sea victory and captured eight of their ships in the Firth of Forth, but Edward failed to follow through with the great land campaign he had promised. When

Richard journeyed to Nottingham to confer with him in October, he understood the reason. Edward was not well; he had the bloody flux. Though he had managed to drag himself up to Nottingham and insisted he would be well enough by next summer to lead the war effort himself, it was clear to Richard that Edward's health was failing. He knew it would be up to him to do what needed to be done.

The New Year of 1482 roared in on a hailstorm. Few celebrated, for it seemed the Four Horsemen of the Apocalypse rode loose across the land. All over England and Europe the harvest had been the worst in many years and starvation exacted a heavy toll with the onset of winter. War and taxation compounded England's suffering. Even Richard had difficulty furnishing his garrisons with enough food. Somehow, against many setbacks, he managed to array an army and as soon as the snows began to thaw he invaded Scotland, burned Dumfries, and assaulted Berwick Castle. Before the end of August, the great fortress on the sea that Marguerite d'Anjou had surrendered to the Scots twenty years before fell back into English hands. Richard sent the news speedily to Edward via a system of relay horses he had set up between Berwick and London. No longer would they have to rely on rumour.

Edward, desperate for good news, was jubilant. As far as Calais, Richard's victory was celebrated with bonfires and he was ordered to appear before the King at Christmas in order to know his thanks. Later that October, a letter arrived from Meg, which Richard read aloud to Anne as they sat in their solar by the fire. It bore Meg's good wishes on Richard's thirtieth birthday and her congratulations on his great victory against the Scots. After expressing her pride in her youngest brother, she included an item of news.

"On the day after the Feast of St. Batholomew," Richard read, "Marguerite d'Anjou died in France in abject poverty, alone except for a few dispirited Lancastrian exiles. Louis refused to believe that all she possessed of value was a painting of the Lilies and Leopards of England that hung over her bed. 'Surely she has a dog?' he demanded. 'Send me the dog.'"

A silence fell. Into Anne's mind rose a vision of Louis XI at their first meeting, sitting on the floor of his filthy bedchamber, in dim candlelight, surrounded by the dogs he had favoured and trusted above all men. She might have found humour in Louis's demand but for its pathos and the memories it stirred; old Percival had died in the spring.

"She was," Anne murmured, "Queen of sorrows and enmities, yet I am sorry for her."

Richard put his arm around her. "The past is dead, dear Anne. Look to the future…"

Anne's gaze went to Richard's bastard daughter, twelve-year-old Katherine, dozing with her head in Richard's lap, and moved to her brother, eleven-year-old Johnnie, playing marbles by the hearth. It touched on George Neville and her uncle John's faithful hound, Roland, stretched out beside him. Then her glance fixed lovingly on Ned, sitting in the window seat, trying to strum a lyre like his father but plucking a host of wrong notes. Percival was no longer curled up at his feet, but death was the way of the world. *In exchange,* Anne thought, *God grants us our young.* She gave a nod, and a smile lifted the corners of her lips.

Early in December Richard journeyed to London to receive his brother's thanks and to confer on future plans. He didn't feel well. He had been plagued by a recurrent toothache these past weeks, but he was moved by the acclaim of the cheering Londoners and the lengths to which they had gone to decorate the city with arras, strewn flowers, and boar banners, and by Edward's near-pathetic gratitude. Court, however, was as foul as always, the air poisoned with suspicions and half-hidden hatreds, and through the glorious pageantry and the varicoloured plumage of tilting knights hissed the endless whispers. Most focused on the King's new mistress, Jane Shore, the wife of a goldsmith, who was beautiful, bright, light-hearted, and witty. And—the whispers claimed—loved not only by the King, but also by the Marquess of Dorset and Lord Hastings.

Richard crossed paths with Jane Shore in the pleasance at Westminster. He was in a hurry to get from the palace to the Abbey when he came upon her strolling between greying Hastings and gaudy Dorset. They did not see him at first, so he had a moment to observe them unnoticed as she laughed merrily while Dorset and Hastings exchanged dark looks over her lovely head.

Richard realised his disgust showed, for when the trio finally noticed him, their demeanour sobered instantly. Jane Shore's laughter died in her throat, and she had the decency to blush as she curtsied while Will Hastings bowed and murmured a genial greeting. Dorset, that contemptible, debauched Woodville, grinned nervously and merely inclined his head in a slight nod, although for insolent Dorset, that represented a great deal. Richard acknowledged them with a curt nod of his own and passed on.

Hastings had met Jane Shore first, the whispers said and, struck by her beauty, had arranged for her abduction—his customary practice for dealing with maidens reluctant to bed him. But the servant woman whom he'd bribed to lure Jane from her house in Cheapside failed him at the last moment. Unable to slake his desire for the young beauty, Hastings wooed her, and in due course, fell in love with her. Edward, noticing Hastings's dejection, inquired as to the cause. Anxious to see the girl with his own eyes, he disguised himself as a merchant and made a trip to her husband's goldsmith shop. More trips followed. Edward, too, was smitten— so much so, that it was said he had distanced himself from Bess. Soon afterwards, old merchant Shore disappeared, but whether he died or discreetly left town was unknown. The affair then began in earnest. And that, whispered the rumours, was when Dorset fell in love with her and she with him, though they kept their passion secret—it was dangerous to cuckold a king.

Richard clenched a fist. Hastings and Dorset had led Edward by the hand down the path of licentious pleasures. They were to blame for the degeneration of the happy valiant prince he had adored into the corpulent, coarse, grim monarch Edward had become.

From the Abbey, where he spent an hour on his knees in silent prayer, Richard reluctantly returned to the great hall where festivities were in progress and took his seat beside his already-drunk brother. Woodvilles were everywhere, lining the High Table, dancing to lutes and viols, clapping for the actors who performed in the pageant "The Agony of Mankind besieged by World, Flesh, and Devil." Edward's five daughters and two sons were present, shining like angels in their brocaded Christmas gowns, but each time Richard looked at the Queen, he saw the half-rotted face of his brother George, now encased behind the altar at Tewkesbury Abbey.

"Louis…" Edward was saying to no one in particular, "has had two attacks of apoplexy… he will soon die! That shall put an end to our worries about Burgundy, indeed it shall." He put the goblet he had been waving around to his lips and wine splashed over his face. He coughed fitfully. Servants rushed to him with gilt-edged towels.

"Sire!" said Edward Brampton, a trusted retainer, striding up. He made a hasty bow. "Messengers from Burgundy, my Liege!"

"Burgundy… Burgundy…" burped Edward. "I cannot give up fifty thousand crowns… Would you give up fifty thousand crowns, Dickon?"

Richard averted his gaze. Brampton flushed. "My Lord, they are not here to ask for aid. They bear urgent tidings."

Richard shifted his gaze back to Edward. He had sunk into his chair and was muttering to himself. "Have them brought in," Richard said. "I will see them." He rose, took up a position beside Edward's chair.

Brampton left the hall and returned with two knights. They knelt at Edward's feet. "Sire, your royal sister, the gracious Duchess of Burgundy, sends greetings," one began. Edward burped. Distressed, the man looked to Richard. At his nod he continued, addressing Richard instead of Edward. "As you know, King Louis of France has swallowed up the Duchy of Burgundy and overrun Artois. Flanders is crumbling before him. Therefore, the Duke Maximillian, unable to find allies against Louis, has had no choice but to make peace with France…"

Richard felt himself turn pale. He looked at Edward. He no longer muttered but sat quietly, listening. Richard was unsure how much he understood, for he made no reaction.

"By this Treaty of Arras, Maximillian has agreed that his daughter Margaret shall marry the Dauphin of France, her marriage portion to be the counties of Artois and Burgundy."

Richard stood rigidly, unable to move. Burgundy, the bulwark of English trade, England's staunch ally, gone, vanished like a phantom into mist. It wasn't possible! He saw Edward in his mind's eye, tall, magnificent, striding triumphantly across the bridge at Picquigny to pick up his French gold. And Louis, shabby Louis, followed by a dog.

Ah, indeed, the spider had woven a fine, silk web...

There was a sudden crash followed by a wailing cry. Edward had upturned one banquet table and was staggering down the dais toward the next, yelling like a madman. Richard rushed after him. He grabbed his arm, but Edward shook him off. Hastings ran to Richard's assistance. Together they managed to take him from the banquet hall, while Edward muttered to himself. Richard finally heard his words: "So many mistakes, Dickon," he was moaning. "Too many mistakes... Louis... John... Bess... *Bess*..."

In the antechamber of the royal apartments, Edward sat weeping. Richard watched, his heart breaking. Laughing, golden Edward, whom he had followed as his lodestar. "What are we going to do, Dickon?" Edward asked in a small voice.

"With Burgundy helpless, we cannot fight France. We must press the war in Scotland to a victorious conclusion. That will secure our border and end the drain on our resources. Maybe we can get the Scots to join us against Louis."

Edward pushed himself out of his chair. Towering over Richard, swaying on unsteady legs, he leaned his weight on his shoulders and looked at him, tears streaming down his cheeks. "I shall have it put before Parliament... Thank you, Dickon, thank you... brother... loyal brother."

Richard helped him back into his chair. He turned to leave. Edward called his name. "Dickon... As reward, I'd gladly give you my crown, but you would not wish to pay its price, brother. You may have anything else you want... Think on it... dear... loyal... brother."

His heart twisting in his breast, Richard nodded.

Anne met him in the courtyard at Middleham. "What is it, my Lord?" she asked, taking his arm and leading him into the Keep.

He shook his head, unable to speak. In their chamber she dismissed Richard's squire and removed his boots herself. A tub was brought in and set before the hearth. She helped him into it. He sat naked on a stool while she gently lathered his body with a soapy sponge. After rubbing him dry, she helped him into a woollen chamber robe and had the servants bear the tub away. She led him to their silken pallet, arranged the cushions comfortably, poured the wine, and served him sweetmeats from a silver platter.

"Now tell me what troubles you so, Richard."

"Edward," he answered miserably. "The loss of Burgundy has practically destroyed him. He'll never see Louis's gold again, nor Burgundy's trade. And before the world Louis flouted the Princess Elizabeth. It has been a harsh blow."

Anne smoothed Richard's damp hair back from his brow. "But he has you to help him recover, dearest."

"I fear he'll never recover," murmured Richard. "He's ill, Anne."

Anne drew his head down against her breast. She kissed his brow.

"Anne... He offered me as reward anything I want."

"Anything?"

"What would you ask for, Anne, if you could have anything?"

She gazed at the fire wistfully. "I'd ask for you. And Ned. And to stay here in the North forever. And never have to go to London again, never have to see court again, never have to see Woodvilles again."

"Aye," murmured Richard. "Aye."

Parliament met on the twentieth day of January, 1483, and granted to Richard and his heirs after him permanent possession of the West Marches, the city of Carlisle, and possession of all Scottish lands he had conquered and all others he could win from the Scots. It was a great county palatine created out of Cumberland County and the Scots Marches, and though it owed obedience to the English crown, it was virtually an autonomous principality. Richard journeyed to London to receive the honour and, exactly a month later, he bade Edward farewell at Westminster and set out for the North. A light snow was falling. As he rode away with Francis at his side, he looked back at Edward, standing in the court, waving him off. It was something Edward had never done before and it filled Richard with foreboding.

"What's wrong, Richard?" Francis inquired.

"I don't know, Francis, but I fear I've looked my last on my brother..." He blinked back his sorrow. *We all make our own choices,* he thought. The Woodvilles had destroyed Edward, but he had not been an unwilling victim. As for himself, there was safety in distance. Perhaps now that he was truly Lord of the North, he and Ned would be safe from Woodvilles. He spurred his horse.

Chapter 12

"And shrieking out, 'O fool!' the harlot leapt
Adown the forest…and the forest echo'd 'fool.'"

*T*he messenger galloped up in a swirl of dust.

It was Good Friday, 1483, shortly before the hour of Nones, and the Gloucester household was picnicking beneath a stately weeping willow on the banks of the River Ure. Anne tensed and held her breath, then heaved a sigh of relief, for he did not wear the royal blue and wine livery of the King but a topaz tunic and the badge of the Black Bull. It was from Lord Hastings that he had come. She took a bite of marchpane. But her happy munching slowed when he drew close enough for her to see his face.

Something had happened.

The man looked more than travel-worn. He looked deeply troubled and weary to exhaustion. He bowed to Richard. "My Lord Duke, I am the bearer of grievous tidings…" He paused, seemed to brace himself. "Your Grace… I deeply regret to inform you, the King is dead."

All laughter died; the minstrels ceased their song. Katherine, picking lilies at the water's edge, straightened. Johnnie, Ned, and young George Neville, playing Knights and Crusaders on the ruins of a stone wall, halted in their steps, and others, in the motion of setting down a game of cards, stilled their hands. Francis turned, his fishing rod limp, and from where he sat on a blanket, Richard stared mutely up at the messenger with unnatural stillness.

It is a tableau I will always remember, Anne thought. She felt as if she were choking. She fell forward and vomited. The action broke the spell that held them. Life breathed back into the statues and they all moved at once. The Countess kissed her silver crucifix and made the sign of the Cross. The boys drew close, and the friends Francis, Rob, and Sir William Conyers encircled the messenger. Richard rose slowly, stiffly, to his feet. He took a step forward, stumbled, and caught at a branch to steady himself. "But his birthday is in two weeks…" was his strangled response.

It was a senseless remark, yet it made curious sense. Edward was not yet forty-three. Not only was his death premature, but he had seemed invincible. The messenger bowed his head. It was the Countess who had the presence of mind to ask, gently, for particulars.

"The King collapsed while fishing, and a week later—on Wednesday, April 9th—he died of apoplexy at Westminster, my Lady."

Richard finally recovered his composure. "Why, sir, does this news come to us from Lord Hastings and not from the Queen?"

"Before he died, the King summoned the Queen's kin and the old nobility to his bedside. Present on one side were Lord Hastings and the Lords Howard, Stanley, and Ferrers, and on the other the Queen's two sons, the Marquess of Dorset and Sir Richard Grey, and her two brothers, the Bishop of Salisbury and Sir Edward Woodville."

Richard waited. An unusual step, to have everyone gathered around at the same moment.

"The King spoke to them at length about his fears for the kingdom and told them that unless they put aside their hatred of one another, his son, and the kingdom, they themselves would be brought to ruin. Lord Hastings and the Marquess were moved to tears by his earnest pleas. They clasped hands and swore to love one another. The other lords followed their example."

"And the Queen?"

"The King did not summon her at the end, my Lord," he said softly.

A bitter taste came to Richard's mouth. *So this was how it ended, this grand passion.* Like a torch to dry grass, it had raged and consumed all in its path until nothing remained but ashes.

The messenger's voice cut into his thoughts.

"The King then dismissed them and summoned his executors, in which the Queen had been replaced by Lord Stanley. He told them there was only one man capable of ordering the realm and subduing the factions that split the court. It was a man he loved well, and whom he knew loved him..." The messenger knelt. "My Lord, the King added a codicil to his will bequeathing his son and kingdom to the protection of his loyal brother Richard, Duke of Gloucester."

Anne cried out, a sudden, choked sound, like that of a wounded bird falling to earth.

Richard swallowed hard on the constriction in his throat. "You have not answered my question. Why then is this message dispatched to me from Lord Hastings and not from the Queen or Chancellor Rotherham?"

The man removed a missive from his pouch and handed it to Richard, who slashed the white ribbon with his jewelled dagger and broke the seal. It was from Hastings. There was no greeting and no signatory.

The King has left all to your protection—goods, heir, realm. Secure the person of our Lord sovereign Edward the Fifth and get thee to London!

"This...?" demanded Richard angrily. "What is the meaning of this?"

"As soon as it became evident that the King was dying, the Queen set about arranging matters to circumvent the King's wishes and rule herself. She has directed her brother, Anthony Woodville, Earl Rivers, to bring King Edward V from Ludlow to London to be crowned immediately."

Richard took a moment to digest the information. Young Edward's crowning in itself meant nothing. Kings had to be crowned. If he were in London, he'd attend to it himself as the first order of business. It certainly did not mean that Bess had to be plotting to subvert Edward's will and set him aside as Protector in order to rule herself. Such a move would have disastrous consequences for the realm, and for Bess herself. Whatever she was, she was no fool. The only possible explanation for Hastings's panic was that hatred of the Queen and her ilk had led him to misinterpret her intentions. Aye, that was it. The matter was a mere tempest in a wine cup. Relief flooded him and he looked at Anne. She was white as the bark of an aspen tree. A fierce anger swept him. He knew Hastings to be wanton, corrupt, and contemptible but he had never thought him reckless before. Reckless, and stupid—to write such foolery! To alarm them in this manner!

"I see no need for rash action. I shall dispatch a query to Earl Rivers in Ludlow, asking by when and by what route the King will travel to London so that I can join them." He waved his hand in dismissal. The messenger bowed his head, but in turning to leave, he lost his balance and almost fell. Richard suddenly realised the hapless man must have lashed his horse the distance and may have barely eaten or slept since he left London. "You have done well, sir. What is your name?"

"Catesby," replied the young man. "William Catesby, my Lord."

"Good Catesby, there is bread and ale and meat; partake and take rest. You need not leave for London until tomorrow. Lord Hastings can wait."

Before many days passed, another messenger arrived from Hastings after Vespers. Richard and Anne had retired to the solar to read Sir Thomas Malory's *Morte D'Arthur* with friends. Richard ripped open the missive. He gave a sigh. Anne placed a gentle hand on his sleeve. "What is it, dearest?"

"Hastings claims the Woodvilles have seized control. Only with difficulty has he managed to limit the size of Edward's escort to two thousand men. He says I should come strongly armed to secure the King."

"Do you believe him?"

"I know not what to believe. There's still no word from Westminster; that does concern me."

"My Lord," said Warwick's old friend Sir William Conyers, "perhaps you should write the Queen and reassure her."

"A good idea. I shall write the council, too."

Richard summoned a scribe and dictated a letter to the Queen expressing his condolences and promising to serve her son as he had served his brother. Then he dashed off another to the council. "I have been loyal to my brother Edward at home and abroad, in peace and in war," he dictated, pacing to and fro. "I am loyal to my brother's heir and all my brother's issue. I desire only that the kingdom be ruled with justice, according to law. My brother's testament has made me Protector of the Realm. In debating the disposition of authority, I ask you to consider the position rightfully due me according to the law of the land and my brother's order." He looked at Conyers. "What think you?"

"'Tis reasonable, my Lord. It reminds them that in appointing his sole surviving brother as Regent—as Henry V did his brother Gloucester—that King Edward was following a custom approved over a century of practice... But a warning at the end might be advisable."

"Add this," Richard told the scribe. *"Nothing which is contrary to law and to King Edward's will can be decreed without harm."* He turned to Conyers. "How is that?"

"The threat should give them pause, my Lord."

Richard rested his hand on Conyer's shoulder. He was a tall man, and the gesture, which had come so easily to towering Edward, felt awkward. He dropped his hand. "Thank you, Conyers. You've always spoken bluntly and advised me well. Let us hope that all the reasonable men in the land don't reside in the North, but that a few are left at Westminster."

A flurry of missives and messengers came and went from Middleham over the next days. Harry, Duke of Buckingham, wrote from his castle in faraway Brecon in South Wales eagerly offering his support and putting himself entirely at Richard's service, with a thousand men if need be. He begged an immediate answer.

Richard wrote back that he was coming south to join the King's procession to London and would be pleased to have Buckingham meet him on the road, but with a small escort only—not more than three hundred. He had decided to disregard Hastings's advice about bringing a strong armed force. Two hundred and fifty men were enough, and if Buckingham brought the same number, they would have more than sufficient escort between them. After all, they were not at war, though it seemed Hastings was itching to start one.

With his friend Francis Lovell at his side, he bade farewell to Anne and young Ned as they stood in the chill, windswept bailey. He was leaving for York, the muster point for his escort, and from there they would go on to London. Anne offered him the stirrup cup. He drank and handed it back to her. She stood on tiptoe to kiss him.

"God be with you and keep you, my dearest Lord," she said anxiously.

"I shall return as soon as matters permit, my dear lady."

She nodded, backed away to allow the children a chance to say farewell. Ned's squire lifted him up for an embrace. "When I'm bigger, my Lord father, you shall not have to ride alone," he said.

Richard tousled his dark hair, not trusting himself to speak. How he loved the boy! Young George Neville stepped forward. "My Lord, I wish you would let me come with you—'tis not too late, even now..."

Richard's lips curved gently. George was eighteen, almost full grown, and nearly as tall as his father had been. With the wind blowing his tawny hair and Roland at his heels, Richard could see John clearly. His heart constricted. "Fair cousin, contrary to what you may have heard, there's no urgency. Attend to my Ned and lady wife, and be of comfort to your dear lady aunt until I return." Young George inclined his head obediently and stepped back.

A silence fell, broken by the loud flapping of the Boar banner in the wind. Then Richard clattered over the drawbridge. His men fell in behind him. As Ned and George waved farewell, Anne stood and watched, gripped by unease. Richard's confidence troubled her. Since he didn't approve of Hastings, he gave no credence to his warnings. Yet Hastings was a seasoned statesman. There was no reason why he would react as he had, if given no cause. Besides, he was kin, married to her aunt, Katherine. It was something they often forgot, since they had been separated by such distances and moved in different circles for most of their life. But kin always looked out for kin.

Her hand sought the gold crucifix at her neck. Richard had many admirable qualities. He was blessed with a fine mind quick as mercury, but dearly as she loved him, he had a fault that could not be overlooked: He had never outgrown a certain childish innocence. *And innocence is dangerous,* she thought, *for it blinds us to truths we do not wish to see.* At that moment a gust of wind brought down the Boar banner in the dale and men rushed to help the standard bearer raise it back up. Anne gasped and her hand flew to her mouth. A portent?

She felt her mother's arm slip around her shoulders. Sorely did she need the comfort! All her life she had read omens in such absurd trifles and, though she always prayed to be wrong, so accurate a harbinger of the future had they proven that she was convinced she had second sight.

Chapter 13

"...the knight...show'd a youthful face,
Imperious, and of haughtiest lineaments."

*I*n York, Richard ordered Requiem masses for the repose of
Edward's soul, then he administered the oath of fealty to King
Edward V to all his men and the city magistrates. There was,
however, one who was absent, and Richard couldn't refrain from
remarking on it when Conyers came striding up to him in the market
square as they prepared to march. "Percy's not here," he said.

Conyer's expression hardened. "My Lord, his messenger said to
give you this." He handed Richard a missive.

Richard read, looked up. "He regrets he cannot accompany me.
His duties at the border require his presence."

"Sounds like a Percy—never there when you need him," said
Conyers, who was related to the Nevilles by marriage, and therefore
suspicious of Percys. He threw Rob Percy a glance, adding hastily,
"No offence meant, Rob."

"None taken," smiled Rob.

Richard mounted White Surrey. "Perhaps this time the Earl of
Northumberland tells the truth... I can vouch that the Scots can
be troublesome."

Near Nottingham Richard found a messenger waiting with a
missive from Anthony Woodville. The Queen's brother wrote that
he expected to be in Northampton around the twenty-ninth of April
and hoped the Duke of Gloucester would meet him there. Reassured
by the courteous tone of Anthony Woodville's letter, Richard sent
back an acknowledgement, relieved that Hastings had been wrong.
More messengers arrived as they rode south. Most came from
Hastings, each bearing tidings more urgent and ominous than the
last. Though Richard was loathe to put any trust in Edward's old
friend, it was becoming more difficult to dismiss Hastings's concern.

"What do you make of this?" he demanded, passing Hastings's
message to Conyers as they rode together in the cool April sunshine.

Conyers heaved an audible breath when he finished reading.

"He doesn't sound like himself," he said, handing back the note.

"Aye, he claims he stands alone, that his very life is in danger because he has espoused my cause. Hard to believe."

"For genial Hastings to make such a statement, the situation must be dire."

"Genial, he is, and brave, too. But dissolute," said Richard with a tightening of his mouth. "There's no reason why matters should be so desperate."

"There's the Queen, my Lord. Her nature is well known."

"She's wilful and greedy, but would she risk civil strife by lawlessly circumventing the King's will?"

Conyers made no reply. Richard gave a sigh. "Only when we are in London and see for ourselves will we know the truth. I shall keep myself uncommitted until then."

"But is that wise, my Lord?" offered Conyers, anxiety evident in his tone.

"Wise, I know not… But it is fair. Perhaps that's more important."

Late on the day Anthony Woodville had expected to arrive in Northampton, Richard rode into the city with his cavalcade. There was no sign of the Queen's brother and young Edward. He dismounted before the inn where he had arranged to meet Buckingham and turned to one of the men he had sent ahead to secure accommodations. "Where are they?" he demanded.

"They have already passed through, my Lord, and continued south, to Stony Stratford."

Richard frowned, looked at Conyers and Francis. "But we clearly had an arrangement to meet here."

They had no chance to respond. The Duke of Buckingham's herald was riding up. The man dismounted, bent a knee. "My Lord, His Grace wishes you to know he will arrive shortly."

"Well then, let's make ourselves comfortable." He turned White Surrey over to his squire and went into the inn, the innkeeper at his heels, indicating the way. Crossing the plank floor, Richard took the creaky stairs up to his room. As he entered, horses' hoofs sounded in the street. "That must be Buckingham."

"Not Buckingham," corrected Francis from the doorway,

"Anthony Woodville!"

Richard went to the window. "Indeed it is, but young Edward is not with him. At least not that I can see from here." He threw his gauntlets on the bed and hurried downstairs.

Anthony Woodville, Earl Rivers, came riding up, surrounded by a train of attendants. "My Lord Protector, I greet thee well! I have come at the behest of our new sovereign King to convey his greeting to his gracious uncle." Anthony Woodville gave Richard a deep bow.

"Earl Rivers, you are most welcome," Richard said pleasantly, betraying none of his unease. "Pray, enter, partake of refreshment." He turned to the innkeeper. "Arrange lodgings for Earl Rivers and his men." He led Anthony Woodville into the parlour. "I see my royal nephew is not with you."

"My Lord, the King pushed on to Stony Stratford for the night because it was feared there were insufficient accommodations for both the royal train and your own." He smiled.

Though Anthony Woodville had tried to speak casually, Richard caught the faint tremor in his voice and knew instantly that he lied. Indeed, if his royal nephew were so eager to greet him, why had he rushed on to Stony Stratford? There might not have been enough room in town for them all, but certainly enough for young Edward and part of his train. Richard decided not to pursue the matter for the moment.

"I see…" he said, inviting his brother by marriage to a plank table in the parlour. Spiced hippocras and appetisers were brought. Anthony Woodville sipped his wine and munched a pasty.

"The ride from Ludlow was most pleasant, my Lord brother," Anthony Woodville said, referring to their ties of kinship through his sister Bess. "I particularly enjoyed the Shropshire countryside. The hills are covered with an abundance of snowdrops this time of year…" He proceeded to paint a colourful account of his journey. They drank together and ate, and for the most part, it was Anthony Woodville who talked. Richard listened, observing him and turning over in his mind the meaning of this cordial embassy that contrasted so strangely with Hastings's reports. Except for one thing—the missing King. That nagged at him.

"...the ceremony was splendid, the King enjoyed it greatly," Anthony Woodville was saying about the Feast of St. George that he had celebrated the night before he left Ludlow. "I remember when our royal brother, King Edward—God assoil his noble soul—made me Knight of the Garter... Ahhh..." He related his memories.

Richard studied him, this patron of Caxton. He certainly did not think of him as kin, and would not address him as brother, but he did not hold him in the same contempt as the rest of his clan. Richard had fathomed the others: they were evil. Anthony was different. His family was tightly-knit, yet he seemed to keep his distance from them. The Woodvilles were worldly, and he, too, enjoyed the good things of life—like the goose liver pate he was now devouring—but he had never displayed the same greed for gold that they had. Indeed, it was said of him that his dress often included a hair shirt. Richard wondered if he wore one now beneath his rich earl's robes of bright blue velvet furred with miniver and trimmed with gold. A smile almost tipped the corners of his mouth at the thought of a pious Woodville. It seemed a contradiction. Even Lionel, Bishop of Salisbury, that large, multi-chinned hog, was a debauched and unholy man.

Aye, Anthony Woodville had undeniably strong spiritual qualities. He debated devotional writings such as those of Christine de Pisane, occasionally indulged himself in a scholarly work of his own making, and had translated three devotional accounts which Caxton printed. He had even penned ballads against the Seven Deadly Sins.

"Have you read Sir Thomas Malory's account of King Arthur's knights?" Anthony Woodville was asking.

"Aye," Richard said, "most recently."

"And your favourite part?"

"When Arthur slays Mordred."

"Why?"

"Justice is done."

"But justice comes at high cost. To get at Mordred, the King must sacrifice himself."

"You miss the point. The cost of treachery is what's high. Justice is all that's left."

"Aha…" said Woodville. Softly, he began to recite, "'Then the king looked about him, and then was he aware of all his host and of all his good knights, no more were left alive…'"

Richard picked up the tale. "'Then the king got his spear in both his hands, and ran toward Sir Mordred, crying, "Traitor, now is thy death day come!"'"

"I pray I never see another battlefield," sighed Woodville. "'Tis too much, all that death."

Now Richard understood why Anthony Woodville had gone on pilgrimage the day after the Battle of Tewkesbury. Edward had called him a coward, this man famed for winning tournaments. He was no coward, and he was no Woodville, this Woodville. He was not a true knight, and not a true pilgrim.

He was an enigma.

Maybe Buckingham would know what to make of him.

Harry Stafford, Duke of Buckingham, arrived in the midst of supper. With a swift movement full of grace and virility he stretched his long legs over the pine bench and sat down. The congenial conversation quickly became merry. Harry Stafford was charming, witty; Anthony Woodville, widely travelled, imaginative. Richard, who felt he could add nothing to their brilliant conversation, listened and said nothing.

It was late in the evening when the three men rose from the table. "So, 'tis agreed we ride to Stony Stratford together in the morning?" said Anthony Woodville.

"Indeed," smiled Buckingham. He slapped Anthony Woodville on the back in a gesture Richard found poignantly reminiscent of Edward. But then, Harry was kin and, after Richard himself, the noblest blood in England. He was descended from Thomas of Woodstock, Duke of Gloucester, the youngest son of Edward III. That Gloucester had been murdered by his nephew, King Richard II. Therefore, when the Lancastrian Henry of Bolingbroke came claiming King Richard's throne, Gloucester's heirs gladly threw him their support.

Richard's gaze dwelled on his cousin. Fair and golden, his features were so perfect, so symmetrical, that the delicacy would have made him too beautiful for a man were it not for his commanding air of self-confidence and the haughty lift of his head. His father and grandfather had died fighting for Lancaster, but that was in the past. Harry was one of them now. He had been raised among Yorkists since childhood and he'd married Bess's sister, Catherine, at the age of eleven. Since this marriage had been forced upon him against his will, his hatred of the Woodvilles was well known, but in the feuds of the last ten years he'd taken no part and was rarely to be found at court. Like Richard himself.

Richard had seen little of his cousin in his life, but clearly their paths had crossed enough at critical times in their lives to shape them in the same mould and forge strong bonds of memory and affection. There was something else. Each time he looked at Buckingham, he was reminded of the blood they shared, for Buckingham bore a startling resemblance to George. He had felt so alone since Edward's death. Now, he thought, gazing at Harry Duke of Buckingham, he was alone no longer.

With a deep bow, Anthony Woodville took his leave. Richard and Buckingham watched as he and his torchbearers disappeared into their lodgings down the darkened street. Richard turned stiffly. Summoning his advisors, he returned to the parlour and resumed his seat at the table with Buckingham. Everyone rushed to join him: William Conyers, Lord Scrope of Bolton, Francis, Rob Percy, and Richard Ratcliffe. Gathered close, they spoke in whispers, faces grim in the flickering rush-light.

"What think you?" Richard asked, his grave question directed to Buckingham.

"We're in a bad situation," said Buckingham, face flushed, blue eyes dark in the dim light. "The King is fourteen miles ahead of us. If the Queen gets hold of his person, she will rule as Marguerite did through Henry, and we are done for."

"Then you believe Hastings—that the situation in London is desperate?"

"Don't you?" Shock widened Buckingham's eyes.

"I don't believe the Queen would risk civil strife by circumventing the Protectorship."

"She stole the King's signet ring and sealed Desmond's death warrant when he wouldn't sign, didn't she?"

"But that was long ago. Age has surely tempered her rashness."

"I have had the distinct displeasure to know her intimately, and I can assure you, Dickon, she has not been tempered one whit. If anything, she's grown greedier, more wilful and thirsty for power. She once vowed to destroy any and all who cross her."

"What about Anthony Woodville? What's his role in all this?"

"Unwilling, no doubt. The Queen has spoken of him disparagingly many times. She's accused him of having more heart for useless learning than for power, and calls him spineless. She's said that he has too many doubts and not enough ambition. In short, he has scruples, and she has none."

"And Anthony Woodville himself, what says he?"

"He's told Bess to show more humility and less pride. His ballads on the Seven Deadly Sins are penned for her…" Buckingham gave a snort of laughter. "But it does no good—she won't read them!"

"Yet in the end, he does her bidding."

"In the end, he is a Woodville."

After a long pause, Richard said, "We cannot fight. We're outnumbered four to one."

"Dickon, there's something you should know." Buckingham shifted on the bench, drew a deep breath. "Years ago the Queen decided whom she would destroy—Desmond, Cook, Warwick, your royal brother George, John Lord Montagu and…"

"Montagu?"

"She planted the idea in the King's mind to take away his earldom. He was a Neville." His mouth thinned. "She has almost come to the end of her list."

"Blessed Mary, you say 'almost.' There are other names on that list?"

"Two." Buckingham leaned across the table. He met Richard's eyes. "Hastings… and you."

Chapter 14

"out...issued the bright face of a blooming boy
Fresh as a flower new-born."

Richard drew back the shutter and looked out at the street. All was well. Beneath the grey skies of dawn, his armed men were in place, guarding the roads and surrounding the inn where Anthony Woodville lodged.

He would do all he had to do, by God! He was no sacrificial lamb to be led to the block like Desmond, and he would not hand Bess the knife to drive into his belly, as George had done. Buckingham had stripped the blindfold from his eyes. He'd been a damned fool to put trust in Bess. To believe she might have learned something from her mistakes, that she might care a whit about the realm. People like Bess never changed, they only grew more embittered with each failed ambition, each perceived slight. She cared only for herself, and her grudges, and settling her old scores, no matter how much time passed between and how much blood was shed. With Bess, time did not heal; it inflamed. She believed Richard blamed her for George's death, and she feared his revenge. She was determined to destroy him first, whatever the cost.

With Buckingham at his side and a company of men at his back, Richard rode hard for Stony Stratford. He found the town crowded with armed men and loaded pack animals. As he neared a small whitewashed inn, young King Edward appeared in the doorway between his half-brother, Sir Richard Grey, and his aging chamberlain, Sir Edward Vaughn. He walked towards a magnificent chestnut stallion, and around him thronged ranks of armed men for whom Richard's own small company was no match.

"Wait here," Richard ordered his men. He spurred White Surrey forward and drew rein before the royal group. They turned. Surprise, uncertainty, and fear flashed across Edward's young face in rapid succession and Richard had the satisfaction of seeing Sir Richard Grey's jaw slacken in shock. If he needed confirmation of Bess's plotting, he had it. The silence throbbed as he dismounted.

Men backed away and opened a path for him. He strode up to young Edward and knelt in homage, feeling their eyes bore into his back.

"My Lord King, gracious nephew, we greet you well and with all reverence," he said.

Edward murmured a courteous acknowledgement while his eyes searched the distance. "Where is my uncle?"

Richard stiffened. *Am I not his uncle too?* "My Lord King, I have grave tidings to relate concerning your uncle Anthony." Richard gestured towards the inn where they could speak privately.

Edward glanced at his half-brother. Richard Grey proved no help. The young man was still struck mute, staring at Richard as if unable to believe the evidence of his own eyes.

"Your Grace, the matter concerning your uncle Anthony is of the utmost urgency," Richard insisted when Edward made no move to re-enter the inn. "May we speak privately?" Again, he pointed the way. This time the young King nodded.

Once inside, Richard expressed his condolences and informed young Edward of the masses he had ordered sung for his father in York and the oath of fealty he had administered to the citizens. He hoped that would reassure the boy of his intentions. His gaze flicked to Richard Grey and Thomas Vaughn, hanging back in the room as if ready to bolt for the door. The exit was blocked by his own men-at-arms, who stood squarely before it. Reassured, Richard turned back to the King.

"Your Grace, your royal father is dead only because certain ministers about his person encouraged his excesses, ruined his health, and brought him to an early demise. These men must be removed from power in order that they not destroy you as they destroyed him."

Richard Grey stepped angrily toward Richard. "How dare you…"

Buckingham blocked him. "How dare you interrupt your betters, Woodville." Eyes flashing, a hand on his dagger, he made "Woodville" sound like an epithet.

As calmly as he could, Richard said, "My Lord, for many years I have served my royal brother in council and in battle. Because of my experience, my reputation, and my nearness of blood, he appointed me Protector of the realm. But these same ministers who brought about my royal brother's death have conspired to set aside your father's will and deprive me of the Protectorship. They are Richard Grey here, his brother the Marquess of Dorset, and your uncle Anthony."

"It's not true!" cried Richard Grey. "Don't believe him, Edward!"

"B-but they are my f-friends and I t-trust them," stuttered the young King. "As for the P-Protectorate, I am certain my uncle Anthony and my gracious mother the Queen…"

"The governance of the realm is for those of royal blood, not low-born Woodvilles!" Buckingham snapped, pushing forward. "Your mother has no rightful authority. You've been deceived!"

Edward paled. His frightened eyes flew from Buckingham to Richard. "B-but what about my uncle Anthony?"

"For my own safety, I've been forced to detain him in Northampton," said Richard. "No harm shall come to him. You can see for yourself when we return tomorrow."

Tears welled in the young King's eyes and he bit his lower lip to stop its trembling as Richard stepped aside to allow him to ascend the stairs to his chamber. Buckingham followed. Richard nodded to his men-at-arms and they seized Richard Grey and Vaughn. He watched as they were taken upstairs. Now he had to deal with the royal escort. He went to the door and hesitated, his hand on the knob. What if they resisted? What would he do? He was outnumbered. He couldn't fight. Everything depended on what he said, and how he said it. He had to do well. There would be no second chance. He braced himself, flung open the door, and stepped out to face the sea of expectant, staring faces.

"The King," he proclaimed loudly, firmly, "has been received into my Protectorship as his father, King Edward IV—God assoil his soul—ordained in his testament. Therefore all servants and men-at-arms who accompanied the royal retinue from Ludlow are dismissed to return to their homes!"

Richard waited. In that moment, life was suspended; he drew no breath, heard no sound, saw no movement.

Then suddenly the world came back to life. Men murmured; horses neighed. Slowly, in small groups they melted away.

Chapter 15

"a blooming boy... crying, "Knight,
Slay me not; my three brethren bade me do it...
They never dreamt the passes would be passed."

Richard returned to Northampton with his prisoners and the King. On the ride back, he stole glances at young Edward. The boy's lower lip trembled and tears sparkled in his eyes, yet he sat erect in his saddle, clinging to his dignity. Richard's heart ached for his nephew. In an instant his life had changed and all that was dear was rent from the young fellow.

He has to be so afraid, feeling so alone surrounded by strangers, not a familiar face among them, Richard thought. He felt guilty about that. To sever all connection with the little King's Woodville past, he'd had to replace young Edward's personal attendants with his own men. He knew that he himself appeared fierce and foreign to the boy, and again he regretted lacking his brothers' casual ways, their brilliant smiles and fair good looks, and their ability to win hearts. He wished he could put Edward at ease, for well he understood the boy's misery. He had been little more than half young Edward's age when his own father died and he'd been sent away for refuge to a strange land; alone, except for George.

He bit down on the emotion that flooded him. He had no wish to be here, to be doing this. But for this boy's mother, all would have been different. If only Edward hadn't married her! But he had. And worse: he had died suddenly, prematurely, consigning England to the uncertainties of minority government and the machinations of an evil Queen. Twice in the last eighty years a child had inherited the throne—Richard II and Henry VI—and each time brought disaster to England. Not for nothing was it said, "Woe to thee, O land, when thy king is a child!"

When they arrived in Northampton Richard sent messengers to Anne and his mother, summoned his secretary, John Kendall, and dictated a letter to Hastings and the council. "I have not captured the King but rescued him and the realm," he began, pacing to and fro. "For those who have tainted the honour and health of the father cannot be expected to have more regard for the youth of the son. For my own safety and the safety of the kingdom, I have arrested Rivers, Vaughn, and Grey and their fate will be submitted to the decision of the council." He halted, heaved an audible sigh. "That is all... Nay, add that I shall soon bring the King to London to be crowned." He waved a hand. "Given under our signet at our town of Northampton, this day, the thirtieth of April, 1483." He threw Buckingham a glance. "What think you, Harry? Is that good enough?"

"It shall make Hastings's work easier for him, I warrant."

Richard went to the window, thrust it open, and peered outside at the armed men milling in the street. Now that his work was done, he felt weary and famished. He hadn't realised how hungry he was or how late it had become. The light was fading fast; it was already five o'clock, high time for dinner. The clanking of dishes and the smell of cooked meat on the spit wafted up from the kitchen, sending his stomach growling.

That evening Richard ate heartily cured tongue, roasted partridge with cold herbed jelly, dates in relish, cheese, waffles, rice cakes, and marchpane. He drank deeply of the sweet spiced wine and noted out of the corner of his eye that young Edward barely touched his food. "Fair nephew, can you not eat?"

The boy shook his head.

"Even kings must keep up their strength." The boy hung his head. "I am sure your uncle Anthony has cleared his plate and would wish you to do the same."

At the mention of his uncle, Edward's head jerked up. "Is my uncle allowed to eat?"

The child's response confirmed what Richard had always suspected: the Woodvilles had poisoned his nephew against him. He gestured to the innkeeper.

"Your Grace?"

"Prepare these same dishes for Earl Rivers and send them to his lodgings."

"But, my Lord, he has already dined."

"Already?" repeated Richard meaningfully. "The exact banquet?"

"Aye, my Lord… Except—except for the rice cakes and marchpane."

Richard gave young Edward a measured glance. "Nephew, I tell you what… If you eat your partridge, I shall send your uncle Anthony rice cakes and marchpane."

The boy picked up a leg and took a bite. Richard watched him. He was nothing like his own Ned, with his fair hair and milk-white complexion, yet in some ways he reminded him of his son. It was his innocence and his vulnerability, for it was apparent that the boy did not feel well. He chewed slowly, carefully, on one side of his mouth, nursing the other as if it were tender.

"Do you have a toothache, Edward?"

Young Edward lifted a hand, gingerly touched his lower jaw on the right side of his face. "I always have pain in my jaw. Isn't a toothache supposed to go away?"

"As soon as we get to London, I'll have my physician take a look," Richard promised, swept with a need to comfort the boy. "He may have just the potion for you."

The table was cleared and more rush-lights were lit. Richard called for pen and paper. Dabbing the quill pen into the ink, he began doodling, one eye on the boy, his mind drifting back to when he'd been twelve himself. He remembered how Edward had appointed him commissioner of array, how Francis and Anne and his friends, the two Toms who'd been killed at Barnet, had insisted he must have a motto. His heart constricted. That had been the start of the troubles, but he'd been too young to understand. All he knew was that he'd been chosen to do man's work, and he was proud. "Do you have a motto, Edward?"

The boy shook his head.

"I do," said Richard. "See…" He wrote out *Loyaulte me lie*— Loyalty binds me—then he signed his name beneath: "Richard of Gloucester." "And you, Harry?" he asked Buckingham.

"Why, indeed, I do!" Buckingham took the pen, dipped into the ink, and wrote out, *Souvente me souvene*. "It means, Think of me often."

"Can you write, Edward?" asked Richard gently.

"Aye," young Edward said with a proud lift of his head. They passed him the parchment, pen and ink. He hesitated. "But I can't write with my left hand, like you, my Lord uncle."

Richard smiled. "A good thing, Edward. Or you would have a handicap to overcome."

Young Edward bent his head. Slowly, carefully, he wrote out his name at the top of the page: "Edwardus Quintus."

Richard examined the stiff, childish hand. "Very good... You know what this means, don't you?"

Edward frowned. "No, my Lord."

"With this signature you can command anything you wish and it will be done, for you are King and your word is law. Is there a desire close to your heart, something you'd like to do? Maybe a gift you'd care to make?"

Edward thought for a moment. "There is a chaplain at Ludlow of whom I am very fond. It would give me much pleasure to reward him."

"His name?"

"John Geffrey."

"Done!" Richard summoned his secretary, John Kendall. "The King commands that you dispatch an order to the custodian of the seal of the earldom of March to send a writ to the Bishop of Hereford asking that one John Jef..." He looked at Edward. Edward said brightly, "Geffrey..." and spelled it out. "That John Geffrey be appointed to the rectorship of the parish church of Pembrigge." Richard looked kindly at his nephew. "See how easy it is, my Lord King?" For the first time, Richard saw him smile.

Later over wine, they read Malory together, and Edward, relaxing a little more, asked questions about kingship and Good and Evil.

"A wise king is just," Richard replied. "When there is justice, all is right with the world. There is peace, men are content."

"Then why was King Arthur and his good kingdom destroyed by evil?"

"Only in Heaven has Good triumphed over Evil for all time. On earth it is a daily battle we wage, each of us choosing our side and accounting for our choice to God on Judgement Day." Then partly to reassure the boy, and partly to plant the seed in his mind by which he might one day judge his own mother's actions, Richard added, "Remember always that the fountain of Goodness is justice, and the fountain of Evil is greed. From greed flows jealousy, hatred, treason, and all foul deeds."

At the end of this heavy discussion, the young King rubbed his bleary eyes and made his way up to bed. And Richard thought, *there's hope after all.*

On the second of May a messenger arrived from Hastings. It was the same man who had brought news of Edward's death. He knelt before Richard. "Catesby, is it not?" Richard asked.

"Aye, my Lord Protector. This time I am heartened to bear good tidings. Your letter to the council was well received. The Protectorate is approved. The Woodville cause has collapsed."

Buckingham gave a cheer. Richard allowed himself a small smile.

Catesby continued. "The Queen has fled into Sanctuary, taking with her all manner of crates, boxes, furniture, plates, tapestries, and coffers containing half of King Edward's treasure. For two days and nights the carts rolled into Westminster Abbey. Lord Hastings bids me tell you that she broke down a wall in order to move in her goods more quickly."

Buckingham roared with laughter. "Last time dear old Bess was in Sanctuary, she complained bitterly of being uncomfortable!"

"What about the Queen's brothers, Dorset, Lionel, and Sir Edward?" Richard demanded.

"Sir Edward has sailed from England with the fleet, taking the other half of the King's treasure with him... My Lord Protector, Lord Hastings wishes you to know that the royal treasury is empty."

Richard sighed. Buckingham laughed. "How very Woodville."

Richard turned his head and looked at him. *Edward would have laughed,* he thought, *and then he would have kissed some merchants' wives and raised more money.* He turned his attention back to Catesby. There was an honest, forthright quality about this sinewy young man who was around his own age.

"You are to be made comfortable and denied nothing, Catesby. Inform our landlord that he is to spread out for you the best table he can prepare, and get some rest. We leave for London at the cock's crow."

Catesby thanked Richard in fine, courtly fashion, adding to Richard's good impression.

Early the second morning after they had left Northampton, the royal cavalcade approached Barnet. The skies were pearl grey, spring flowers dotted the bright green rolling hills, and the air was damp with dew. Bells from Hadley's church chimed for Prime, flooding Richard with memories. Many who rode with him this day had fought against him that other, but there was one he missed still… One he would always miss. Halting before the peaceful little church on the hill, Richard dismounted and went inside. He leaned against the pillar, laid his hand against the cold stone. The nave was gloomy and cool; candles flickered at the altar and feeble daylight bathed the Cross.

As he stood there, twelve years slipped away in his mind and again it was the day of the Battle of Barnet, a day of death. He heard the crash of metal, the screams of terrified horses, the cries of dying men. The fog swirled around him. Swords flashed; men fell. Cries of York and Lancaster mingled in the murk. He closed his eyes and saw himself dismounting before Hadley Church after the battle. Looping the reins of his war horse around a tree at the edge of the graveyard, he had followed its curving path to the entry. With great effort, he pulled open the iron-hinged parish door. The church was empty. A fitful grey light came through the coarse glass windows, and the dank, musty air stank of burning mutton fat from the votive candles at the altar. He had taken a step down into the nave and felt suddenly faint. Putting out an arm, he had leaned heavily against a pillar.

Drawn by the clanging of the door, a pimply acolyte had come out from the vestry. He had given a start at the sight of Richard.

Richard had suddenly realised how frightening he must appear with his bloodied hair and clothes, his bloodstained, bandaged arm, and a face that had to be as pale as a phantom. His taut mouth had softened.

The boy had recovered, and come towards him. "Do you seek Sanctuary, my Lord?" he had asked, recognising Richard's high estate despite the condition of his clothes.

Richard had been unable to respond. He was fighting a terrible fatigue, a pounding head and blurred vision, and stood erect only with great effort. He had rubbed his eyes in a desperate attempt to clear his mind. *One day,* he had thought with a stab of fear, *the moment will come when I will no longer be able to exert will over body and I will break.* He had shaken his head with determined effort. "Priest!" he had demanded, more harshly than he intended. The flustered boy had run off into the nave and out the west door into the churchyard. A moment later an older man had lumbered in the same entrance. He was gaunt, his grey hair thinning around his tonsure.

"My Lord, you asked for me?" he had inquired, his face flushed.

With a slow, clumsy motion, Richard had withdrawn a small bag of coins from within his doublet. The movement had sent pain shooting along his right side. He grimaced.

"Pray, sit down, my Lord!" the priest said. With concern for his benefactor, he dusted the steps with a corner of his gown.

Richard shook his head. "I wish… prayers… Masses… for one dead in battle." There were many dead in battle whom he would remember: his boyhood friends, the two Toms; his squire, John Milewater. And Warwick. Later, he would buy Masses for them, too, but this—this could not wait.

The priest took the purse, made the sign of the Cross. "It shall be done, my Lord," he had said. "And the name of the deceased, God assoil his soul?"

"John Neville, Marquess of Montagu," Richard had replied in a choked voice. "He died honourably." Somehow, he felt it necessary the priest know that. Heaving himself around, he had dragged himself from the little church.

A voice said, "May I help you, my Lord?" It was a different priest than the one he remembered.

Richard bought masses for the repose of John's soul. Outside, in the brightness of day, he breathed deeply of the fresh morning air. Aye, life went on. He strode to his waiting horse. It was Sunday, the fourth of May.

Chapter 16

"He makes no friend who never made a foe."

The gates of London stood open to receive them. Men jostled for space on the city walls and cheering crowds packed the narrow streets and hung over balconies. Gaily dressed in scarlet trimmed with fur, the Mayor came out to greet Richard and the young King, accompanied by his aldermen and a train of leading citizens, including five hundred eminent merchants clad in violet. All across the city, church bells pealed in celebration.

Richard and Buckingham rode bareheaded. They had both dressed in coarse black mourning cloth and their men had donned black for the occasion, making a sharp contrast with the Londoners. Young Edward rode between them, dressed in blue velvet with a matching cap crowning his bright hair. Richard thought him a touchingly diminutive figure on his enormous chestnut stallion. On through the narrow streets rolled their procession, past Ludgate, past St. Paul's, around Westminster. There was such a noise of welcome that Richard knew Bess had to be drowning in it, even through the thick stone walls of her sanctuary. He couldn't suppress a smile. On this day, the odious Queen had planned to have young Edward crowned, and then, no doubt, to sign his death warrant.

Young Edward was temporarily lodged at the Bishop of London's palace. With Buckingham at his side, Richard went to Crosby Place, his townhouse on Bishopsgate Street, where Hastings awaited. The reunion was warm. Richard's disapproval of his brother's friend had evaporated under a weight of gratitude for his recent services. Francis and Rob joined them, and over wine and sweetbreads, they brought one another up to date.

"A great deal has happened. The people are afraid, Dickon," said Hastings.

"I know. To ease their minds, I'll have the city fathers and the lords spiritual and temporal take the oath of fealty to King Edward in a public ceremony as soon as possible."

"A good idea," agreed Hastings.

"Aye," Buckingham agreed, "but one thing troubles me. Edward needs to be moved from the Bishop's Palace. It's not suitable housing for him."

"What do you mean?" demanded Hastings. "It's perfectly suitable for a King. Henry lodged there many a time."

"That's exactly the point, Will. We don't wish to remind the people of Henry. He was deposed."

"No one's planning to depose Edward, Harry," said Richard.

"We know that, but others don't," insisted Buckingham. "Besides, it's not safe."

"It's as safe as anywhere else," Hastings replied irritably.

Buckingham turned to Richard. "Dickon, you know I'm only looking out for your good. The Woodville bitch is hatching plots to get her hands on Edward even as we speak! Edward must be moved to the Tower."

"If you do that, Dickon, the people will see young Edward as your captive," Hastings said.

"Nonsense!" exclaimed Buckingham. "The Tower's a royal residence! The bitch chose it for Edward's birthing, remember? Warwick's revolt forced her into Sanctuary. That's why Edward was born at Westminster instead of at the Tower. Besides, there's a zoo to entertain him. He'll be happier there."

"I'm inclined to agree with you, Harry... Rob, Francis, what do you think?" Richard asked.

"Harry makes a good case," Francis said. "I vote for the Tower."

"So do I," Rob agreed.

Rob and Francis brought up other business, and when they had covered everything of importance, everyone relaxed amiably until the subject turned to Bishop Morton.

"I hear you were doing well with Edward in Northampton, but Morton ruined everything once you got here," Rob said.

Richard put down his wine cup, said bitterly, "Morton told him that his mother had fled into sanctuary on my account." He bit his lip. "The devil take Morton!"

Hastings gave him a sympathetic look. "Edward had to know sometime, Dickon."

"But not like that. You should have seen Edward's face. Now he thinks I'm the villain the Woodvilles have always claimed. Not only did I lock up his brother and favourite uncle, but his mother fears for her life at my hands." He rose from the table, went to the window and fidgeted with his ring, as he always did when he was nervous or upset. A silence fell. Rob and Francis shifted uncomfortably in their chairs, but it escaped Richard's notice that Buckingham's expression turned suddenly fearful and that he fell into deep thought.

Hastings set his cup down and heaved a sigh. "Aye, by fleeing into Sanctuary, Bess Woodville proclaimed her own guilt to all the world but him." He felt badly for Richard, who was in an awkward position. It would not be easy for him to regain the King's trust after this. For himself, however, he was vastly relieved. He'd had no part in the events at Northampton—at least not in young Edward's eyes. That was what counted. One day the young King would no longer be a minor. Richard had, at best, five years to change the boy's mind. With Bess around, that might not be enough. As there was no comfort to offer, Hastings brought up the delicate matter he had put off. "Bess is not without her sympathisers, however. You do know that Edward's Chancellor, Archbishop Rotherham, delivered the Great Seal into her hands in Sanctuary?"

"I heard," replied Richard wearily. "A damned fool thing to do." Rotherham would have to be disciplined, and the sooner, the better.

Shaken from his reverie, Buckingham snorted. "He must be charged with treason and thrown into prison!"

"That's too severe. He meant no real harm, and he did return to reclaim it," Hastings replied. "He's a friend of mine, Dickon, and I've promised him I'd speak for him. He told me it was her tears that drove him to it. Will you consider a pardon—"

"Not bloody likely!" exclaimed Buckingham. "He's a Woodville lover. And you're the fool, if you think we'll let him off!"

Hastings' face registered surprise, then anger. "He's served Edward well all these years. The man's old and doddery. Bad judgement—not treason—is all he's guilty of." He twisted around, looked at Richard. "He has his supporters. I believe it would be a mistake to deal harshly with him. With all deference, Dickon, I have more experience in such matters than Harry!"

Richard pushed open the window. God's curse, how he hated court! Already the feuds were breaking out, even here, among his own. Why had Buckingham spoken so rashly and insulted Hastings? They could have come to an amicable agreement. As it was, each was waiting to see whom he would favour. He agreed with Buckingham that the offence could not be overlooked. Rotherham was one of the Queen's men and owed his rise to her influence. The fact that he gave her the Great Seal proved it, and he had demanded its return only because he realised he'd backed the wrong cock in this fight and feared for his own hide. But now, thanks to Buckingham's damned intemperate remarks—for which he'd have to rebuke him later—it was impossible to discipline Rotherham without offending Hastings. And he owed Hastings. If it hadn't been for him, he'd be dead now.

"We can't overlook his action," said Richard, "but stripping him of the chancellorship should be enough." He held up a hand to silence Buckingham's protest. "He can still remain on the council. I was thinking of the Bishop of Lincoln as his replacement. What do you say, Will?" John Russell, Bishop of Lincoln, was one of Edward's most accomplished diplomats and a man of great learning and piety.

Hastings had always been a generous man, and generously he accepted the compromise. The tension was defused. But no sooner had he left than Buckingham turned his fury on Richard. It took Richard far longer to mollify him.

Rob and Francis, watching silently, exchanged glances. The future did not bode well. There was going to be trouble between Hastings and Buckingham.

The next day Richard held his first council meeting. He included even those who had supported the Woodvilles. This was no time for confrontation. He had to heal the divisions if they were to avoid strife. He knew civil war too well; it set brother against brother and friend against friend, and was the greatest horror, the deepest agony, a land could inflict on itself. "What is past, is past," he said in the Star Chamber at Westminster, named for the tiny silver stars emblazoned on the blue silk cloth that lined the walls. "Let us learn from our mistakes and move forward to a prosperous and glorious reign."

The council took up debate and set the date of Edward's coronation for St. John's Day. The only serious problem that confronted Richard was what to do with the Woodvilles. His feelings of magnanimity had evaporated since it was discovered that Richard Grey had three wagonloads of armour and weapons in his train. Clearly, they had been planning to use force. Even now Bess's brother, Sir Edward, was defying the government with his fleet. And her son, Dorset, who had managed to escape from Sanctuary—no doubt with the aid of that bawdy woman Jane Shore—was trying to raise men against Richard's Protectorate.

"On the matter of Anthony Woodville, Grey, and Vaughn, I wish charges of treason be brought against them." These accursed Woodvilles cared nothing for England. They would plunge the land back into evil days to secure their base of power. He wanted them to pay the full penalty: *Death.*

"My Lord of Gloucester," said beady-eyed Morton in his slippery voice, his lips barely moving, "you had not been appointed Protector at the time. Therefore, there was, in fact, no treason."

"Their intention was clear. They tried to set aside my royal brother's testament and my Protectorate in order to seize power and rule the land themselves. That is treason."

"You say they *intended* to displace you, my Lord of Gloucester. Their intent is a matter of conjecture. Treason is a serious charge. We cannot convict on mere hearsay about intent when there is no proof whatever… I motion that they be released immediately for lack of evidence."

A bitter argument ensued. Howard and most of the barons readily concurred with Richard, but Hastings, former chancellor Rotherham, and the spiritual lords sided with Bishop Morton. A consensus was finally reached. No charges were to be brought, but Anthony Woodville, Grey, and Vaughn were to be kept in confinement. As for the Queen, she was to be offered pardon if she would leave sanctuary and promise to behave honourably, as befitting a Queen Dowager. A committee was appointed to negotiate with her.

"What about Sir Edward Woodville and the ships he's taken?" demanded Hastings.

"We won't have to use force if we pardon his men," said Richard.

"But how do we get the offer to the sailors?" asked Chancellor Russell. "They are at sea, and no ship could get close enough to announce it."

Richard looked at the man he'd nicknamed "The Friendly Lion" in childhood. "Lord Howard, what say you?"

All eyes turned to the portly magnate in dark blue brocade. The hero of the Scots invasion rose to his feet. If Richard was the first general of the realm, Howard was its admiral, but though the sea was his coinage, he fought like the silver lion of his blazon both on land and sea, and it was Towton that had distinguished him. That, and his unwavering loyalty to York for over two decades.

"It can be done," said Howard. "And I know just the man for the job, my Lord."

The hint of a smile tipped the corners of Richard's mouth as he voiced the name. "Edward Brampton, who captured St. Michael's Mount from Oxford."

Howard hitched up his gilt-embossed girdle from below his ample belly and grinned. "Indeed, my Lord. There's ne'er a sea dog in the land as hardy and resourceful as Brampton. He'll pull it off, by God!" He winked. "And if anyone wishes a wager on it, my lords, I'll give 'em ten to one odds..." He looked around hopefully. No one accepted his wager. His acumen in turning a profit was too well known. He not only fought in ships, he traded in them. Over the years, he'd managed to grow many a penny into a pound.

By the end of the week, in a dazzling display of swashbuckling bravado, Brampton managed to get the message to Woodville's men, who then plied their guards with drinks, overpowered them, and sailed for London. Edward Woodville, left with only two ships, fled to Brittany. But he took with him half the King's gold.

During the course of the next few days Richard confirmed many appointments and made new ones. Hastings kept all his offices. He was still Captain of Calais and Lord Chamberlain of England, which gave him ready access to the young King's ear. Hastings's messenger, William Catesby, who had served them so well during the momentous events of the past weeks, was appointed chancellor of the earldom of March.

But unknown to Richard, Hastings chafed.

He had expected to be Richard's right arm, as he had been Edward's. Had he not stood alone against the Woodvilles? Had he not risked all—his very life, in fact—to warn Richard and prepare him to thwart the Woodvilles? But for him, Richard would not be Protector. And now that he was, Richard had turned all his favour, all his attention, all his trust, to that upstart, that rash, brash, ebullient, unstable George-like Buckingham. In council Buckingham was the dominant voice. Wherever Richard rode, Buckingham rode at his side. Richard had loaded Buckingham with titles, lands, and offices. Buckingham was Commissioner of Array and Constable of all the royal castles in five counties, Steward of all royal manors and demesnes. Buckingham was Chief Justice and Chamberlain in North and South Wales, Governor of those regions, Constable, Steward and Receiver of most of the Welsh castles. The list went on and on, the result being that Buckingham was the virtual ruler of Wales, the Marches, and most of the West Country.

And Hastings was not happy.

Even Jane Shore, for whom he had hungered all these years, and who had finally come to his bed after Dorset's disappearance, could not console him with all her beauty and all her wit.

Chapter 17

"—a man of plots,
Craft, poisonous counsels, wayside ambushings—"

"I bear dire tidings," said the black-clad messenger from Middleham. "My Lord Protector, I regret to inform you that your gracious nephew, George Neville, is dead."

Richard felt as if his breath solidified in his throat. "How...?"

"He was thrown from his horse. His neck was broken."

Slowly, heavily, Richard let himself down into a chair and listened to the man's report. Riding to Nappa Hall near the falls at Aysgarth to visit their neighbour, old Metcalfe, and hear his tales of Agincourt where he had fought with Henry the Fifth, George's horse had stumbled. He had been flung headlong to his death.

"Leave me," said Richard.

There was a sudden commotion at the door. Rob's voice called out, "Richard..."

He looked up with bleary, unfocused eyes. "What is it?"

"Are you ready to see them now—the petitioners, I mean? The hall is full. The line reaches almost to the river."

"Tell them to go away and leave me in peace. In peace, do you hear!" He leapt to his feet and pushed past a stunned Rob, making for the chapel.

First the father; now the son. Richard's head throbbed. He fell to his knees before the altar. For most of the day, a dismal rain had been falling. He stared up at the gilt cross glinting in the gloomy light and remembered the cross at Hadley Church. He had stopped at Barnet on his way to London. It had been the fourth of May. George had died that sunny morning. Maybe even as he was passing through Barnet; maybe even as he had stood gazing up at the cross at Hadley Church.

A shiver ran down his spine. He found the knowledge ironic, and horribly unsettling.

Arrangements for the coronation moved forward. Under the watchful eye of the Keeper of the Wardrobe, tailors fashioned splendid costumes for the young King and his household. Meanwhile, the full council continued to meet formally in the Star Chamber while smaller committees assembled in the Tower to issue the writs and bills necessary to the state's business, or met at private homes for informal consultation.

Richard's own intimate circle of advisors gathered at Crosby Place. They included Buckingham, Francis and Rob, Howard, Conyers, and the Lords Scrope of Bolton and Scrope of Masham, who were Neville kinsmen and had been good friends to John. There was also one newcomer to court: Richard's nephew Jack, the young Earl of Lincoln, his sister Liza's son. He had grown up since the day he'd won the prize of a pup sired by Percival for committing to memory verses written by his great-grandfather, Geoffrey Chaucer, and he was now twenty years old, anxious to help his uncle in any way he could.

The pace of these days was gruelling; the tension draining. Crosby Place bustled with Richard's household staff, his growing number of supporters, and the daily procession of men with special grievances or hopes for favour. In the city he had always hated, there was no joy for Richard without his family, but duty called, and Richard had never failed the call of duty—even in the face of grief.

Late on a Thursday evening, exactly a month after George's death, Anne arrived at Crosby Place, escorted by a pale and drawn George Gower. Rain had been pouring all day and she shivered in her wet clothes. Richard removed her soaking mantle and embraced her. He rested a gentle hand on Gower's drooping shoulder, met his pained eyes. "We'll miss him, Gower."

"Aye, my Lord," Gower managed.

Richard swallowed his sorrow and led Anne into the solar where a fire glowed. "How is Ned?" He was distressed to find her looking thinner, her eyes red-rimmed. Young George's death had exacted a heavy toll.

Anne shook her damp curls. "I wish I could say he was well,

Richard, but he misses George... Ned fell ill on his birthday, you know, two days after George..." She broke off, struggled for composure. "That makes two fevers in one month. It is so worrisome."

Indeed, young George's death had reminded them of the fragility of life. Richard caught her hands in his own and looked steadily into her eyes. "Remember what I keep telling you, my little bird?"

"'Richard liveth yet,'" Anne repeated dutifully. "I realise you were a sickly child, and so was I. But 'tis... difficult, Richard."

"I know, my love." He drew her to him and smoothed her wet hair. "Yet all will be well in the end, God willing." He kissed her on the brow. "Now eat and get some rest. I have to take care of business for a bit, but I'll hurry along as much as I can."

"Oh, Richard, must you? You look tired, my love. Can you not take this one night off?" Indeed, he looked quite exhausted. He was pale and hollow-cheeked. If he had lost weight during these two months, he had also lost sleep, for there were bags under his eyes. She traced the line of his jaw lovingly. "We can curl up before the fire and take a bath together."

Richard was sorely tempted. Gladly would he have dismissed everyone and committed to the morning the business that remained, but he could see that Anne was more fatigued than she knew. Rest was what she needed, maybe even more than he needed the comfort of her arms.

"Nay, my love, I can't," he said gently. "There is business I must attend tonight."

Forcing a light note into her tone, Anne said, "Then you owe me."

"Will you accept a promissory note?" Richard grinned.

Anne smiled, stood on tiptoe and gave him a kiss on the cleft in his chin.

Richard stood warming his hands at the hearth in his bedchamber for there was a chill in the air though it was summer. He'd spent nearly the full day in council attending affairs of state and so busy had he been that his meals were brought to him. As a result, he hadn't seen Anne all day, but it was precisely to spend time with her that he'd pushed himself so hard. Now it was past Vespers, candles had been lit, and the remains of dinner cleared. Almost all the urgent business had been concluded. Only one other matter remained.

As he waited for Buckingham, Richard poked the glowing embers with a cherry branch, Hastings on his mind. He didn't wish to believe that the man with whom he was linked by so many memories, with whom he'd shared the desperate flight to Bruges and the bloody battle in the fog of Barnet, that the man who'd hated the Woodvilles as much as he and loved his brother as much as he, was now turning against him for jealousy of Buckingham.

Once Richard had thought that he could never forgive Hastings that night in the Leicester brothel and the death of the maiden he'd abducted and raped. He realised now that he had forgiven him long ago, and the subtle change in Hastings's behaviour troubled him. Hastings must have been troubled himself. Four days earlier he had requested a private meeting at Westminster in a secluded chamber far from the main passageway. Dismissing the servants, he had shut the door carefully before airing his concerns. Strictly speaking these were not in the plural, for they all reduced themselves to one problem: Buckingham. What began as an amicable discussion ended with both of them shouting at one another. The turning point came when Hastings said it was a damn fool thing Richard did, to entrust so much power to Buckingham.

"I can't understand how you can be so blind to the faults obvious to everyone else! Why do you think Edward never gave him responsibility?"

"Because Buckingham hates Woodvilles and Bess had Edward's ear."

"Because Buckingham's ambitious and he can't be trusted!" Hastings had declared.

"He's given me no reason to doubt him. He's stood by me from the first."

"So have I!"

"And he didn't vote against me on the matter of the Woodvilles."

Hastings was taken aback for a moment. "Aye, I did vote with Morton, for the same reason as the others. Because young Edward is King, and by executing his favourite uncle I'd be condemning myself in his eyes. That I'm not willing to do. When you're in a marsh, you take care where you step. It's a matter of survival. What's commonly known as statecraft!"

"I've heard that word before. It doesn't replace principles."

Hastings looked at him strangely. "As Edward said, you see everything with a moral squint. He once accused you of being naive. That alone can be deadly where you stand. To that, I'll add another charge. You're a bad judge of character, Dickon, and too loyal for your own damn good. You trust the wrong people and don't see their faults until it's too late!"

Richard was enraged. Hastings had attacked him on two fronts: his honour, and his loyalty. "Admit it, Will—you're jealous, that's the real problem here!"

Hastings's face had changed. "There's no more to be said."

Richard had watched him leave.

Relations between them had been strained ever since. Not until then had Richard realised that he cared for Hastings—Hastings, who had proven his loyalty to York all the years of his life, who had loved Edward as much as he himself, and who had managed with his humour and his generosity to win Richard's own heart in spite of himself.

Voices in the stairwell interrupted Richard's thoughts. He heard Buckingham's merry laugh. He put down the cherry branch and turned to see him stride into the room. Carefully, in a manner reminiscent of Hastings at Westminster, Buckingham shut the door and met his eyes. When Buckingham's first words gave voice to his own fears, Richard knew he could not run from his concerns any longer. "I must warn you, Dickon, Hastings has something afoot." He threw his cloak aside and reclined on the settle.

"Our spies looking for Dorset report that Hastings has been meeting frequently with Rotherham, Morton, and Stanley. The meetings are at night and kept so secret our men have been unable to learn their purpose... One thing is sure, though. It's not to conduct the business of the council. Hastings has never been one to sacrifice his leisure for affairs of state."

True enough, thought Richard. *And neither are Morton*

nor Stanley.

"What troubles me is that Rotherham is included in these meetings. He's the Queen's man. I've no idea why you went so easy on him, Dickon."

Richard threw Buckingham a sharp glance. If Buckingham had his way, everyone would go to the block. Richard had warned him to watch his temper and not to be so high-handed with the others. As expected, Buckingham hadn't liked it much and had a few hot words for Richard himself. Now he acted as if he'd forgotten the whole episode. Richard decided to ignore his remark. Buckingham could be volatile and stubborn, and sometimes he didn't listen, or he heard only what he wanted to hear. It would be pointless to confront him now and indulge in old arguments when so many new troubles awaited.

"Rotherham's a Woodville dupe, but I'm more concerned about Morton," Richard said. "He's a man of plots and venom. Yet we must win them over, for the sake of the realm." He stroked the embers again. The years since Picquigny had confirmed Richard's opinion that power, not God, drove Morton. Edward had trusted him, and for Edward he had performed well. Morton had imagination and a clever mind, and the vast experience of his sixty-odd years, which had taught him when to be bold, and when to be prudent. But there was something about him that reminded Richard of Louis XI, that sly, wily, devious master plotter. He put the cherry branch down. "Then there's Stanley."

Warwick's erstwhile brother-by marriage, Lord Stanley, was a survivor, a man who had deserted his allies time and again, yet always managed to wriggle back into favour. Marguerite, the Duke of York, Warwick, and Edward had all shared the dubious honour of having been betrayed by Stanley, not once, but several times. Each time they not only forgave him, but heaped him with honours.

"Stanley stands for Stanley. One thing we can rely on, as surely as spring follows winter, is that Stanley will ride at the winner's side, no matter what his sin. Not for nothing is he called the Wily Fox... Aye, Harry, I know what they are, those three. But Hastings..." Richard gave a sigh, shrugged his broad shoulders. "He's profligate. He was responsible for my brother's debauchery.

I've long despised him for that. Yet I like the man, Harry."

"Everyone likes Hastings. That's why he's dangerous."

"We must not be rash. Let me think on it."

"Don't take too long." Buckingham rose from the settle. "They'll no doubt make their move before Parliament meets on June 25th. That's less than three weeks away." He picked up his cloak and strode out.

Richard went to the window and gazed at the dark night. Torches appeared in the court, followed by men's voices and the clattering of horse hoofs as Buckingham trotted out. The gate banged shut. Richard sighed inwardly. Another decision to be made; so many all of a sudden, and no time to reflect, to weigh the pros and cons. He had always hated making hasty decisions, yet now there was no time for anything but haste. A gentle touch on his arm interrupted his thoughts and a soft hand slipped around his chest. Warmth suffused him. "Anne," he whispered, turning to enfold her in his arms. She had slept late this day and the rest had done her good. A touch of colour had stolen into her cheeks and her eyes were brighter.

"I'm calling that promissory note you gave me yesterday." She smiled. Her arms encircled his neck and she pressed her soft curves into the hard, lean contours of his body.

"Anne… Anne…" he murmured, his mouth crushing hers hungrily. "How I've needed you… How I've missed you."

Anne shivered with a giddy sense of pleasure. Roughly he swept her up into his strong arms and carried her into the bedchamber. A burning sweetness engulfed her and she returned his kisses with the same growing desperation. Richard blew out the candle by the bed and his lips recaptured hers, more demanding this time, and they made love with an urgency they had not known before. They were, Anne thought as she sank and resurfaced in the flow of passion, like two drowning souls in a violent rainstorm of vivid lightning and wild winds. Then her thoughts fragmented and she abandoned herself to the turbulence of passion, clinging to him in the darkness until all was still again.

Chapter 18

"The world's loud whisper breaking into storm."

*L*ate the following evening Lord Scrope of Bolton knocked at the door of the royal apartments with the announcement that Robert Stillington, Bishop of Bath and Wells, wished a word with Richard on a matter of utmost urgency.

Anne's violet eyes widened. "At this hour, Richard? But it's almost Compline."

"I assure you, if the old man has dragged me away for anything less than a treasonous plot, I'll wring his scrawny neck." Richard grinned as he rose, but Anne drew him back to the settle.

"Why would Edward's old chancellor wish to see you now? You showed him no favour after Edward took away my uncle's chancellorship and gave it to him. Stillington was no friend to us."

"Or to Edward at the end. They quarrelled and Edward dismissed him, just as he did your uncle. The old man was a bit too friendly with George. That probably had something to do with it."

"I remember now... Wasn't he imprisoned in the Tower at the same time as George?"

"Aye, for defaming the King, but I know not what he said. Now I must go." With great reluctance, he released her hand. "Best you not wait up for me, dearest Anne." *Maybe it is the lateness of the night,* he thought as he strode down the dimly lit passageway, or maybe merely that he was tired. But he was gripped all at once by an inexplicable unease.

Richard stepped into the small parlour where Stillington awaited.

"What's so important that I must be disturbed at this hour?" he said, disguising his discomfort with anger.

Stillington cleared his throat nervously. He clutched an agate rosary that was looped at his waist, and his hands shook so violently that Richard could hear the small stone beads chattering against one another.

"My Lord Protector, I have long been in possession of an inflammable secret, one I should have cleared from my conscience years ago, but I dared not... I dared not, you see... Now, I must. The time has come, indeed it has. It cannot go on any longer..."

An inflammable secret? What is the old man babbling about? Stillington had fallen silent. Richard waved a hand impatiently. "Speak, then!" Fear and fatigue made his tone harsher than he intended and the old man gave a start.

"If you remember, my Lord, your gracious brother the Duke of Clarence—God have mercy on his soul—was executed in the Tower immediately following a private meeting with the King." His words were coming in such a rush, they almost slurred.

"Aye," said Richard sharply, wishing he wouldn't dredge up these painful memories.

"You may also recall that the next day I was imprisoned in the Tower?"

"For three months," said Richard curtly. He didn't feel well all of a sudden. His head throbbed from lack of sleep and the gruelling pace of the past weeks. He eyed the chair in front of him longingly, but if he sat down, he was afraid he might never get up. He moved to grip its carved back.

"'Twas because he found out what I knew, and he—God assoil his soul!—told the King. 'Tis for that he died and I was imprisoned in the Tower on pain of death. Not until I vowed never to speak of the secret again and paid a..." the Bishop flinched, "hefty fine was I granted a royal pardon."

A thin smile came to Richard's lips that even now the memory of the fine was as painful to the Bishop as his loss of freedom. "And this inflammable, expensive secret?" Richard prompted, almost playfully. He was feeling strangely light-headed, as if he'd drunk too much hippocras.

The Bishop made the sign of the Cross. "May God Almighty forgive me for breaking my oath, but I do it for the peace of the realm... My Lord Protector, the children of Elizabeth Woodville and King Edward are bastards because King Edward was wed to another when he married the Lady Elizabeth. You are rightful heir to the throne."

Richard almost burst out laughing. What nonsense had the bishop conjured up in his old befuddled head. "Is this a jest?"

"No jest, my Lord. I should have spoken earlier. I should have... I didn't and it cost the realm much that is on my conscience."

Stillington's face was drawn tight in a solemn expression at once determined and fearful. He had the look of a man who spoke the truth, Richard thought. Yet it was not possible.

Or was it?

He blinked to clear his rampaging thoughts. "Repeat what you said."

"My Lord, neither King Edward V nor his brother, Richard of York, have rightful claim to the throne. Their father, King Edward, was married at the time he wed Elizabeth Woodville."

"Who was this lady?" Richard mumbled thickly, his heart pounding. He tightened his grip of the chair.

"Lady Eleanor Butler, widow of Sir Thomas Butler and daughter of Talbot, the Earl of Shrewsbury. Her father-in-law, you may remember, was Lord Sudeley."

Richard felt the blood drain from his face. A terrible tenseness pervaded his body. He leaned his full weight on the chair, feeling as if he clung to the edge of a cliff. This was no light-love that could be dismissed, but the daughter of an earl. And not just any earl. The great John Talbot himself, the Terror of the French...

"Lady Eleanor was newly widowed when your royal brother became King. They met after the King seized Sir Thomas's two manors which Lord Sudeley had settled on her when she wed his son. She appealed to King Edward for restoration of the manors, which he did."

"What proof do you have of this accusation? I will not take your word on it!"

"Nay, you need not, my Lord Protector. I have proof." From deep within his robes, Stillington removed a small leather pouch. He took out a yellowed piece of parchment and passed it to Richard.

Richard snatched the letter. He examined the broken seal closely, dropped into the chair and read. The breath went out of his lungs in one long, audible gasp. There was no doubt; it was Edward's own seal, in his own handwriting, in his own words, ordering

Stillington to come to Lady Eleanor's private manor in Shrewsbury to perform a ceremony of marriage. And it was dated February 12, 1462. So reminiscent of the facts as they had been with Bess was it, that it had the ring of truth. Richard pushed himself out of the chair.

"The Lady Eleanor," Richard asked, blinking to focus his vision, "where is she now?"

"Dead, my Lord. She went into a nunnery immediately after the marriage between the King and Elizabeth Woodville was made public. Her heart was broken and she had no will to live. She died but four years later, in June 1468."

Edward's words came drifting back to him across the years: *I cannot if I would... I go in alone.* Edward had been hiding something, he'd known it even then. In a flash sudden as lightning out of a summer sky, all the fragments came together and the picture they formed was hideous. He had never known his brother. Edward had not only been debauched and deceitful, the murderer of a saintly King and of a brother—all of which Richard had accepted and forgiven—but he had been truly venal, the flower of wickedness. He'd sacrificed family and realm to his lust for a woman not only unfit to wear the crown, but without the right to wear it. He'd never repudiated her, not even when it became clear that she worked evil, and would always work evil, as long as she remained Queen. Had he confessed the truth while he was still alive, all could have been mended. Now...

Richard pressed a hand to his brow to steady his dizzy head. Now the path to the future was obscured, rocky, forked, and more treacherous than he could ever have imagined. There would be those who would never believe, no matter what proof was offered. If he set his nephews aside, there could well be another civil war. He would give his own life to see that didn't happen. Whether he exposed Edward's bigamy or whether he chose to bury it, it had to be the right decision. One that would avoid bloodshed.

"You are not to say a word of this to anyone. You understand, to *anyone!*" He scarcely recognised his own voice.

Stillington nodded, clutching his rosary even tighter. "But my Lord Protector, you will take the throne, won't you?"

"I know not, Stillington… I know not."

"My Lord Protector. You must! You cannot refuse—the crown is yours by right! You are the only one who can save us!"

The old man's eyes betrayed his terror. Aye, the Woodvilles would make short shift of him once they gained power. Of him, and them both—and many others. He turned away to the window, exclaimed in a voice filled with anguish. "Leave me, Stillington! Leave me to think. God knows, I need time to think!"

Anne awoke in the middle of the night to find that Richard wasn't there and that she had been crying in her sleep. The dream had awakened her, not the gargoyles of her childhood. There had been several of those lately, but this dream was new, tender in many ways, and all the more painful because of it. In the dream she had been picnicking on the banks of the Ure. Ned and young George Neville were laughing and dropping lilies into her lap, while her mother smiled and Richard strummed his lyre and sang, *Blow trumpet, for the world is white with May! Blow trumpet, the long night hath roll'd away!*

Then in the dream, Edward had come, tall and shining, stretching out his hand with a gift of shining fruit—luscious dark cherries and a purple plum. She had chosen the plum, and when she tasted it, a heavenly sweetness had flowed through her until a woman's clawed hands snatched the cherries from Edward and flung them away, and then she saw that they were not cherries at all, but blood from the severed head of a boar. The sweetness in her mouth turned to bile, and she leaned forward to vomit. And awoke weeping.

Its significance was not lost on her. In Edward's gift of the West Marches, the county palatine created out of Cumberland and the Scottish lands, her dream of a place in the North far from court, had come so close to attainment—so close—that she had felt its light shine on her face for one bright, brief moment. Then Fortune had plucked it away.

Anne sat up, pushed back the heavy velvet bed curtain, and groped for her slippers. She slid her feet into them and threw a blanket around her shoulders. She went to the window seat. The garden was bathed in moonlight. All seemed serene.

The garden lied. In this place of intrigue and deceit, even the moonlight lied. How she missed the North. How she missed Ned! How she missed young George! She'd had him buried not in the Neville vault at Bisham Abbey, but at Sherriff Hutton, so he could remain close. Ned had loved him like a brother, and sick as he was, had insisted on visiting his tomb. Together they had knelt by the cold stone, and wept, and prayed. But there was no respite from the grief. Selfishly she had fled Middleham as soon as Ned had recovered from his illness, hoping to flee her grief as well. *Oh, Blessed Virgin, it didn't help!* Wherever she went, she would never be able to forget that handsome young face, forget that he'd been the last of the Nevilles. Others bore the Neville name, but what did it matter when they didn't carry in their veins the blood of her father and uncles? That line was dead, trod into dust. There would be no more John Nevilles, no Richards, Thomases, or Georges named in their memory to bear their blazon, to look back on them.

There was Ned, of course, but he was a Plantagenet, like the other sweet Edward who'd come to live with them. Bella's boy. He bore her father's title, Earl of Warwick, but in no other way did he resemble the magnificent, confident baron who'd been his grandfather. Her heart constricted. Poor little lad. He'd been given into Dorset's care after his father's death and Dorset had abandoned him at one of his manors in the West Country. The boy had even been denied the company of his sister who had been sent elsewhere to live these past five years.

Dorset has much to answer for, Anne thought. Under his care, Bella's son had grown into a shy, frightened eight-year-old who spoke with a stutter, if he spoke at all, and who seemed—maybe due to neglect—to have difficulty not only communicating, but comprehending. It was all Edward's fault. How she hated him for what he had done! Not only to George's little Edward for putting him into the care of a Woodville, but to his own little Edward for putting him into the hands of his maternal relatives and turning his heir into a Woodville, one who cringed with loathing and fear whenever Richard approached! And not only for that. She hated him for what he had done to her father, to her uncles, to Richard—

to England! While he cavorted and drank and turned a blind eye to the feuds that infested his court, the price of his marriage to Bess Woodville had been paid in blood. Now his negligence had bequeathed them a terrible legacy.

A future of fear.

She looked up at the moon, which was nearly full, gleaming silver white. She looked back at the garden that was bathed in its light. All she saw were the shadows.

Chapter 19

"Here are snakes within the grass."

*R*ichard contemplated the future, unable to forget the past. Unable to forget that Thomas, Duke of Gloucester, who helped govern during the minority of Richard II, was savagely murdered by his nephew for his pains. That Humphrey, Duke of Gloucester, Henry VI's uncle, had been murdered by men who had turned the King's heart against him. Yet neither had done what he had done. When young King Edward reached the end of his minority, where would the Protector run for protection?

Mass the next morning was nearly insufferable since old Bourchier, the Archbishop of Canterbury, never one for clear thoughts and concise language, droned on ceaselessly. The moment it was over Richard bounded out of the Abbey, turning heads and raising eyebrows as he hurried across the garth to the royal apartments of the Palace. In the Painted Chamber where his closest friends and advisors had gathered, he dismissed the servants and barred the doors. Then he disclosed Stillington's secret. Howard, Rob, Francis, Jack, the Scropes, and Conyers had misgivings initially, but were of one mind in the end. Richard had to take the throne. Only Buckingham had no doubts whatsoever. He was jubilant.

"Why this gloom?" He poured wine for himself, grinning broadly. "We're not at a funeral. This is a celebration!" He downed a gulp, smacked his lips, and surveyed the others. "Let's drop the pretence and admit that what we dared to wish has become our legal right. We all know the realm needs a man, not a boy. A land ruled by a minor is a land torn by faction. I, for one, burn to serve you, Dickon, not some Woodville bastard. And you have no choice but to take the throne. For England's sake—if not for mine, or your own!"

"What if others don't agree with you, Harry? What if they resist? Civil war's a price I'll not have England pay."

Buckingham appeared taken aback. "Then sound out the lords of the realm," he said, recovering. "If they're willing to support you, there's no problem, is there? And Dickon, remember as you contemplate whether or not to accept the throne, that dukes of Gloucester have a habit of coming to bad ends. It's worse for you. Bess would not let your boy live."

"Call a meeting," said Richard.

The full council met in the White Tower the next morning, promptly at ten o'clock. Stillington gave his statement. Each member examined Edward's letter with utmost care and passed it to the next. Debate opened fiercely and raged from ten in the morning until two in the afternoon. Most of the lords—spiritual and temporal—were satisfied that Stillington spoke the truth, and the majority wished Richard to immediately proclaim it to the people.

"No," said Richard. "We must test the minds of other lords, prelates, and men of influence, even commoners. We can have no dissension. If I take the throne, it will be with the consent of the people."

Then Richard rode the barge back to his Crosby house. The sky was overcast and it was hot and humid. Flies buzzed in his face and the dank river smell offended his nostrils. *Court is like this,* he thought. *Rank and vile, a breeding place for vermin that would suck one's blood dry if given the chance.* He mopped his face and neck with his handkerchief. As soon as his barge tied up at King's Quay, a messenger rushed to him.

"Can this not wait?" Richard demanded, not slowing his pace as he crossed the landing dock and took his horse to Crosby Place. He dismounted in the cobbled court and ran up the steps into the house with the messenger in hot pursuit. A path opened for Richard through the crowded hall, then closed again, cutting off the messenger. A thousand voices rang in his ear, begging a moment. *Damn them all, I need a moment!* A moment to change his damp shirt, a moment with Anne. A moment without people clinging to him, stealing the air from his lungs, infecting him like some poisonous vine—without messengers waiting to hand him dire tidings of death, and secrets, and plots!

"My Lord..." panted the messenger, catching up with Richard as he strode into the private quarters of the house. "The Duke of

Buckingham is most anxious you receive this report without delay!"

At the sound of his name, Buckingham emerged from a chamber in the hall.

"How did you get here so fast?" demanded Richard, finally halting.

"I rode the distance and brought him with me. He missed you at Westminster. Wait till you hear what he has to say!"

"I could happily wait forever," said Richard, striding into the chamber.

"Then you'd be done for, Dickon—good as a cooked boar." Buckingham grinned as he shut the door. Richard pulled off his gauntlets, threw them on a sideboard, and sank into a chair.

"Jesting aside, Dickon, this is no light matter. This man's been assigned the duty of watching Jane Shore." Buckingham waved a hand and the messenger spoke.

"My Lord, Jane Shore became the mistress of the Marquess of Dorset as soon as the King fell ill."

Richard heaved a weary sigh. There was nothing new here. Lewd conduct was to be expected from such a woman and they had already suspected this. Impatiently, he loosened his collar.

"When the Marquess vanished, she began a liaison with Lord Hastings, whom she met again while visiting the King at the Tower..."

Richard stiffened. "She visited my nephew at the Tower?"

"Many times, my Lord. She has no children of her own and 'tis said she is fond of King Edward's children."

"Then there is nothing here of any great importance."

"My Lord Protector, from the Tower Jane Shore went to visit the Queen..." Remembering Richard's command that the Queen henceforth be called by her first husband's name, he said, "Forgive me, my Lord, I mean Dame Grey—in Sanctuary."

Richard froze. Buckingham threw him a meaningful look.

"Jane Shore... Jane Shore," Richard muttered angrily. "Jane Shore loves Dorset, then she beds Hastings, then she visits Bess." He leapt to his feet. "So that's it! That's how it has come about. Jane Shore has turned Hastings against us, Harry, probably at Dorset's bidding. Hastings, that fool—that crazy old dolt—how could he espouse his cause with that of Bess Woodville?"

"Desperation, Richard... Desperation drives Hastings to the Woodville witch, as surely as it drove Warwick to the Bitch of Anjou."

"But doesn't he see, the stupid fool, that Jane Shore loves him not? That when the Woodvilles gain control, Bess—evil as she is— will destroy him? Doesn't he see that they're using him for their own ends?" And Hastings had accused him, Richard, of blindness and bad judgement!

"He's in love. He's ambitious. He sees what he wants to see."

Richard sagged against the wall, feeling suddenly sapped of strength.

"Surely now, *you* see..." Buckingham warned, "that you can wait no longer?"

Richard pressed a hand to his aching head.

It was Tuesday, the tenth day of June, two weeks from Edward's coronation. "We have a problem," said Richard, glancing around the table at the faces of his closest advisors. There was Howard, Francis and Rob, his own kinsmen Buckingham and Jack, and the Neville kinsmen Conyers and the Scropes. His secretary, John Kendall, with whom he had forged a close bond of friendship during these days and nights of frenetic activity, sat at his writing desk, scribbling notes. "We must ascertain whether there's a conspiracy in the making." He related the facts of the case.

"Surely Hastings's loyalty is not in question? It's not possible Harry!" said Francis.

"You can't deny the facts!" retorted Buckingham.

"We have no facts, Harry. Only suspicions," said Richard.

The debate raged for an hour. Then Buckingham rose to his feet. "You must act, Dickon. You cannot afford to wait and hope that all will be well. You're accessible to the plotters—their armed retainers throng the city. If they choose to seize you, you may well be unable to fight them. To delay until the plot is proven could be fatal!"

"But to condemn a man before we ascertain his guilt—that would be lawless murder."

There was a knock at the door. It was Sir Richard Ratcliffe, the Yorkshire knight and brother by marriage to Richard's friend Lord Scrope of Bolton. "My Lord, an urgent message has come for you from Lord Hastings."

Glances were exchanged around the table. "Show the messenger in," commanded Richard.

Ratcliffe hesitated. "My Lord, he states that his message is for the ears of the Lord Protector alone."

"Very well, I'll see him in my private chamber."

Moments later he stood stiffly while William Catesby knelt at his feet. He motioned him to rise. "What is Lord Hastings's message?"

William Catesby flushed. "My Lord, it is not *from* my Lord Hastings that I come, but *about* him."

"What do you mean?"

Catesby cleared his throat nervously. "This is not easy for me, Your Grace. Lord Hastings has been good to me. But I am a lawyer, and the law is all that holds back tyranny and anarchy. When men go wilfully against the law, no good can come of their actions…"

"Speak, man. What's on your mind?"

"My Lord Protector, your life is in danger. There is a conspiracy by the lords Rotherham, Stanley, Morton, and Hastings to seize the government from you and put you to death!"

Richard felt the blood drain to his feet. It was the nightmare of Edward's court reborn; all the licentiousness, the corruption, deceit, and hatred of faction against faction. That was what they wished to bring back—that misery, ugliness, and evil. God's curses on them!

Then the heaviness in his chest receded, gave way to fierce anger. "Follow me!" He stormed back to his council. "Tell them, Catesby!" He stood seething while Catesby delivered his report. Gone were his doubts. To avert civil war, to save his life, to uphold the will of the dead King against the faction of power for power's own sake, he had to act, and act quickly, as he had at Stony Stratford. That single stroke had undone the Woodvilles without a drop of bloodshed, for it had been sudden as the fall of an axe. There was no other choice.

Chapter 20

"the Powers who walk the world
Made lightnings and great thunders over him."

On Friday the thirteenth of June, the Feast day of Corpus Christi, Richard strode into the White Tower and took the stairs up to the council chamber only a few doors from young King Edward's royal apartments. The Thames sparkled brightly in the fine summer sunshine, making his eyes ache, and the church bells that solemnly clanged the hour of ten heightened his unease. He had summoned the plotters to a meeting. They were all present when he entered: Hastings, Stanley, Bishop Morton, and Archbishop Rotherham. Richard was in no mood for preamble. The events of the previous day weighed heavily on his mind and he had barely slept, for the dragon of his childhood nightmares had returned with its red eyes and fiery breath to keep him tossing and turning through the night. He took his place at the head of the table without a word while his friends, Buckingham, Howard, Francis, and Rob distributed themselves among the empty chairs. With a rustle of gowns and a crosscurrent of greeting, everyone took their seats.

"My Lord of Gloucester, you seem quite pale this morning. Are you unwell?" inquired Morton. "Perhaps these strawberries will help. I brought them for you from my garden." He indicated a silver platter of large red strawberries at the centre of the table.

This slippery cleric sounds so genuinely concerned, Richard thought, *I'd be fooled if I didn't know better.* He ignored Morton and his strawberries, looking instead at Hastings's broad-carved face sitting at the opposite end of the table. Bright sunlight slanted over his brother's friend in uneven rays, making his expression hard to read. Hastings was fifty-three now, his hair heavily sprinkled with silver, yet he was still a fine looking man, erect and broad of shoulder, his eyes still clear blue and his smile rakish. Richard wondered if he had come fresh from mistress Shore's bed. His mouth thinned with disgust.

Hastings shifted in his seat and his face came suddenly into sharp focus. He had no smile. His eyes were hollowed, his mouth twisted. His normally florid complexion had taken on an odd greenish tinge, as if he were going to vomit.

He hates what he's done, Richard thought with a momentary softening of resolve. Then he stiffened. *But he would have killed me anyway.* Richard rose to his feet. Abruptly, he said, "Good men died at Barnet and Tewkesbury, at Towton, Sandal, Ludlow, and St. Albans. I need not name all the battles; you know them as well as I. But I will tell you why they died. They died because of greed—greed, which is the root of all evil. Greed, which breeds injustice, jealousy, ambition..." His mouth contracted. His eyes travelled around the table and rested on Hastings. "And treachery."

"Your Grace, with all deference," Morton said, "while I concur wholeheartedly with your sentiments, we came this morning to council, not to church." He gave a chuckle. Old Rotherham's sour mouth curled in his long narrow head and Stanley leaned back into his chair, but Hastings made no reaction. He was staring down at his hands and seemed distracted.

"What exactly, my Lord, is our first order of business?" demanded Morton, shifting his large mound of blubber in his seat.

"Our first order of business, Dr. Morton, is exactly that." Gripping the edge of the table forcefully, he directed himself to Hastings. *"Treachery."* Hastings jerked up his head. Their eyes met.

"A conspiracy has come to light against the government," he resumed. "Bess Woodville and her adherents are the ringleaders. Chief among these is Shore's wife." Hastings's face twitched with pain and he looked away. "There are others." A deadly silence fell. "You, Stanley, and you, Morton... and Rotherham here..." He swung on Will Hastings. "And you, Hastings, have plotted with the Woodvilles for my downfall!"

Stanley went a blotchy red, Rotherham squirmed in his seat like a worm exposed to sunlight, and Morton sat still as a beached whale, his stony dark eyes on guard, watching carefully.

"Nay, my Lord!" Hastings gasped. "I deny it!"

"You fought with me at Barnet and Tewkesbury, my Lord Hastings. You even fought at Towton, and still you were willing to plunge England back into the black strife of civil war!" Richard dug his fingernails into his palms so tightly he drew blood. "If I didn't have proof, I never would have believed that you, of all men, could, for greed, throw in your lot with the Woodvilles when you know what they are, what they'll do!"

The colour drained from Hastings's face. He rose heavily. "What proof can there be? I am no traitor. My entire life has been devoted to York."

"The others I can understand," Richard went on as if Hastings hadn't spoken. "We all know their mettle! But *you*..."

From Stanley's side of the table there came a shouted curse and a shuffle as he reached for his dagger. Francis was too quick for him. Lifting his arm, he struck Stanley's wrist from below, sending the dagger flying into the rushes on the floor. In the motion of rising, Stanley lost his balance and fell, striking his head against the edge of a chair. The others sprang to their feet. Rob flung the chamber door open with a cry of "Treason! Treason!" Armed men rushed into the room. There was a brief scuffle. Stanley was pulled to his feet and Hastings was seized, along with his fellow plotters. Richard said, "You demanded proof. Catesby is my proof."

Hastings's mouth fell open and all his breath came out in one audible gasp.

Richard felt a sharp, sudden anguish. "How could you, Will—how could you do it?"

"I had no choice. You gave me no choice, Dickon."

"I see. In what way, exactly, was I responsible for your treason?"

"You shut me out, you listened only to Buckingham—a man as twisted as George ever was, and as hungry for power."

"Jealousy has driven him mad!" Buckingham cried. "Traitor, how dare you?"

"You and your glib tongue and your pretty ways—you're carved in George's image and you'll bring naught but misery to those who trust you!" Hastings turned his tortured eyes on Richard. "You wouldn't listen to me, Dickon, and you haven't the craft to rule yourself. You see only black and white—you're as Edward said you were: naive, too damned honourable, blinded by ideals. You can't accept that those days are over, if they ever were at all. You're like the unicorn—rare and admirable—but you won't outrun the dogs!"

"And you, Will? When you did become one of the dogs? Once you had ideals yourself—you understood loyalty. Never did I think that you, of all men, could end up playing traitor!"

"And I never thought to see the day come when you, of all men, could end up plucking the crown from your brother's son! Tell me, Dickon, which of us is the traitor here?"

Richard went rigid. He looked along the table into the sudden silence, into Hastings's eyes, staring accusingly back at him, into the faces of the others. The room seemed to fracture, shatter into fragments, then it steadied, pieced together. He stared along the table and the blood pounded in his head, his heart hammered in his breast, sweat trickled down his brow. His eyes went to the captain of the guard standing at Hastings's side. In a tone hard as flint, he said, "Take this traitor away and strike the head from his shoulders."

A horrified gasp went around the room. Hastings cried, "What about a trial? I'm entitled to a trial!"

"You're entitled to nothing, traitor!" seethed Richard, his face a glowering mask of rage. "You stand convicted by your own words. There is no need of trial."

Hastings jerked around in his captor's arms, turned his terrified eyes on Howard. "Jack, for God's sake, tell him I'm entitled to a trial—speak for me!"

"My Lord, I pray you reconsider," pleaded Howard. "What need is there of such haste?"

Richard slammed a fist hard on the table. "There is need! There is…" A sudden, agonising pain shot through him. With great effort he lifted his throbbing hand and motioned to the captain of the guard.

Hastings squirmed. He opened his mouth to protest, but no words came, only a terrible choked sound. The captain hesitated. "My Lord Protector—where shall it… it be done?"

"The green!" barked Richard.

"But… but we have no scaffold…"

Slowly, ominously, Richard turned his head, his grey eyes stormy. "Then use a log," he muttered.

"Aye, Your Grace, aye!"

Hastings was hurried from the chamber and the others taken into confinement until it could be decided what was to be done with them. Richard fell into a chair. Dimly through the open window he heard shouts calling for a priest. An unnatural quiet fell. Memories flooded him: Hastings laughing with Edward, making fun of Henry at Middleham; Hastings in Bruges, at Barnet, at Tewkesbury. Hastings, his beloved Edward's loyal friend. Everyone liked Hastings. He liked Hastings. That's why it hurt so much, why it was so hard. Why it had to be done quickly. For if it were not done quickly, he could not do it at all.

An eternity passed. More shouts arose in the courtyard. No one moved but Buckingham, who went to the window as Hastings was led to the green by the Tower chapel and his head rudely thrust onto a log intended for repairs. Buckingham watched the axe rise, and watched it fall, marvelling as he always did at the quantity of blood that gushed from a man's severed neck. He waited until Hastings's body had ceased its ghastly twitching, and then looked at Richard. He had slumped over in his chair. He went to him and rested a hand on his shoulder.

Word of Hastings's execution reached Crosby House within the half-hour. Concerned for Anne, Rob Percy galloped to tell her. He found her in the hall standing at the window with her ladies, looking anxiously at the crowds that had gathered outside the walls. Without a word he took her elbow and steered her into Richard's bedchamber. His look sufficed as dismissal for the servants. The door thudded shut. Anne stared at Rob's ashen face, full of hard tidings. She stiffened, instinctively reached for the bedpost. Rob delivered his report.

"Richard… he'd never… never do such a thing," Anne managed, "such a terrible thing… You have it wrong, Rob. Putting a man to death without trial—Hastings is kin, my aunt's husband! No, Blessed Virgin, he couldn't do it! It's not possible…"

Rob was looking at her with pity. She tore her eyes away from him and her frantic glance went to the window. "No!" she cried. "Not without a trial, with only a log to serve as block…" Her stomach heaved. She felt the bedpost slipping from her grasp. Rob's strong arms seized her, held her, steadied her. "How could you let it happen?" she whispered, breathing hard. "Why didn't someone stop him—why didn't you, Rob?"

"I wanted to, Anne. We all wanted to. But we couldn't. It had to be done, for the sake of the realm. If he'd waited, he could never have done it. He knew that himself. He acted in anger, but it was the only way. Hastings would not stand by and let Richard take the throne, whatever Richard's right. He was mounting a powerful resistance and the land would have been torn by fighting. Richard couldn't let that happen. He had no choice, Anne."

"But—but can he live with what he's done?"

Rob made no answer.

Chapter 21

"Ay, ay, O, ay—a star was my desire"

An hour after Hastings's execution, Richard sent a yeoman of his household to fetch the Mayor of London, Edmund Shaa, to the Tower. After appraising him of events, he had John Kendall draft an order for the executions of Anthony Woodville, Richard Grey, and Thomas Vaughn. Taking the pen with his left hand, Richard dipped into the black ink and carefully signed *Richard of Gloucester* in his strong, clear, evenly spaced script. He entrusted the death warrants to Sir Richard Ratcliffe, the loyal knight who had discharged himself so well the previous week when he'd borne Richard's letters to supporters in the North. Happily, there had been no need for those reinforcements after all. London had stayed calm. "Anthony Woodville is to be informed that, because of his sister's plotting, he is condemned to death," said Richard.

"Aye, my Lord," said Ratcliffe.

Richard glanced up to see the captain of the guards standing at the door. He flinched. The man paled.

"My Lord," the captain said nervously. "I come for your instructions on the disposition of the traitor's body. Is his head to be displayed on London Bridge?"

"No!" Richard drew a thick breath, averted his gaze. "The body of the Lord Chamberlain is to be borne to Windsor and there buried in the unfinished chapel of St. George, close to King Edward's own tomb, as my royal brother had wished." The captain bowed, turned on his heel, and was gone. Breathing hard, Richard leaned his full weight on the table, bent his head.

Kendall rose from his writing desk. "My Lord…"

"I'll be all right, Kendall." He drew another deep breath. He was drained with fatigue, yet it was early, only midday. He reasserted the discipline of a lifetime and when he spoke again his voice was steady. "Make a note, Kendall. You are to prepare a letter to Lady Hastings as soon as time permits…" He broke off, reminded of something he had forgotten. That Hastings was not only a friend, but kin. His wife was Warwick's sister, Katherine Neville. Anne's aunt. He swallowed.

Kendall pulled out a fresh sheet of parchment.

"Offer her my protection. Tell her I am granting her all her husband's lands and the custody of Lord Hastings's heir until the boy comes of age. I also grant her the wardship of the young Earl of Shrewsbury, who is married to her daughter." Was that atonement enough? Would Hastings's widow forgive him what he could not forgive himself? He paced. "Then draft a proclamation to the people. Inform them of Lord Hastings's treason and his beheading on the Tower Green. Tell them there is no cause for alarm. The government is secure. Tell them Hastings was an evil councillor to my royal brother, King Edward, that he enticed the King to debauchery and vicious living..." For a moment, a vision of the young maiden that Hastings had raped at Leicester flared in his mind. She had been around twelve years old, Anne's age at the time, barely older than a child. He halted. "Add this," he said. "That this very night past Hastings has lain with Shore's wife, who was herself one of the plotters."

If he kept reminding himself how debauched Hastings was, maybe it would help.

Exhausted from lack of sleep and the traumatic events of the day, he went with Francis to his mother's home of Baynard's Castle where Francis lodged. It was closer to Westminster and he would not have to face Anne there. The hour was late, past matins, by the time they arrived. The household slept but he and Francis both knew sleep was a luxury which would be denied them on this night of nights.

"Treason," Richard murmured over a cup of wine in his bedchamber. "I remember the first time it reared its hideous head... At Ludlow, when my father's captain, Trollope, defected to Marguerite taking our battle plans with him. Marguerite's men burned the town and raped the women." He gulped wine and slammed the cup on the table. "Once upon a time, honourable men would rather have died than play traitor. But evil times beget evil ways."

"Have you decided what you'll do with Morton and the rest?"

Francis asked.

"Imprisonment for Morton; a pardon for Stanley."

"But that's too lenient! Stanley's a time-server. You'll never be able to trust him."

"By showing goodwill, maybe we'll win goodwill."

"Execute Stanley! He's proved himself an enemy."

"I can't. Buckingham's interceded for both Stanley and Morton. And Scripture preaches forgiveness, doesn't it?"

"You'd be better served to be more ruthless. A king is his sword, Richard. I fear that by refusing to wield yours, you'll encourage treason with your leniency."

Richard lifted his eyes to Francis with effort. "The truth is simple, Francis. I've no stomach for more bloodshed. I must atone for Hastings's death, that's why I'll spare the rest—though none of them are half the man he was. I'll keep Stanley at my side where I can watch him. He's a wily bastard, that one."

"What about Jane Shore?"

"She'll do public penance by walking the street with a lighted candle, and then imprisonment. For a short spell."

Francis smiled faintly. "A bit mild for treason, wouldn't you say? But, then, you never could be hard on women. Richard…"

"Aye?"

"Have you decided yet whether you'll make Stillington's disclosure public?"

Richard knew what Francis was really asking. Whether he'd take the throne. He shook his head, ran a hand through his hair helplessly. "I thought I knew. Now I'm not sure."

"You must," said Francis. "Not just for England or yourself. But for Ned… For Anne."

Richard frowned. Ned, for obvious reasons—if Bess didn't kill him, he would end up like George's poor boy, abandoned and abused, frightened half out of his wits. He crushed the thought. But Anne? "Even Bess wouldn't execute a woman, Francis."

"There are worse things. Have you forgotten what they did to Humphrey of Gloucester's wife?"

Christ, how could he have forgotten? Charged with witchcraft, forced to do penance through the streets of London, she had been imprisoned for life on the Isle of Man!

"Or Bess might force Anne to marry a man she chose for her."

Richard gave a groan, dropped his head into his hands.

Francis hated what he was doing, but someone had to strip Richard of hope, make him face reality. Only then could he overcome his nature and act against himself, against the loyalty that still bound him to Edward. For if he didn't take the throne, what in God's name would become of England? "The best to be hoped for is that she'd be confined into a convent for the rest of her life."

Richard raised his head, looked at Francis with stricken eyes. "All I ever wanted was to serve Edward."

"I know, Richard... I know."

"It isn't fair!" Richard said suddenly, surprised to find himself voicing the old cry of his childhood. He had forgotten it in recent years. "It just isn't fair."

At Buckingham's request, Bishop Morton was sent to Buckingham's castle of Brecknock in Wales for confinement, and Stanley was restored to his place on the council. There was still one major embarrassment for Richard that required his attention.

Bess.

Since Richard felt he lacked the eloquence with which to present his case persuasively, Buckingham addressed the council when it convened at Baynard's Castle on Saturday morning, the day after Hastings's execution.

"Her behaviour is an insult to our government!" Buckingham declared in his mellifluous voice. "By remaining in Sanctuary she is proclaiming to the world that she has cause to fear us, when nothing of the kind is true..." He cut a fine figure in his tunic of white and gold brocade sewn with gems and fur-trimmed azure velvet mantle. On his golden curls sat a matching blue velvet cap ornamented with a pearl and ruby brooch. He sparkled as he moved with easy grace, and every eye was riveted on him.

"How many times have we offered her our sworn word and assurances that if she removes herself from sanctuary, she will be afforded every protection and honour due a Dowager Queen? 'Tis not fear that keeps her there." His bright blue eyes blazed around the chamber. "'Tis malice!" The few *Nays!* were drowned out by a large chorus of *Ayes!*

"Be that as it may, we can do nothing about the former Queen. However, her son Richard of York is a different matter. He must be secured from Sanctuary. The King needs his brother's companionship. The King needs his brother at his coronation. If Prince Richard does not attend his own brother's coronation, the ceremony will be blighted by his absence—just as the spectacle of Bess Woodville hiding her children in Sanctuary blights our government in the eyes of Europe!"

Hearty *Ayes!* met this comment.

"Since the Woodville Queen is unwilling to give him up, let us take him from her by force. A nine-year-old child needs no sanctuary and is not capable of wanting sanctuary. Therefore he can be removed without violating the holy right."

Cheers erupted, followed by a huge clamour as everyone began to talk at once. When the voices finally calmed, a vote was taken. The spiritual lords were divided, but the temporal lords sided with Buckingham. The boy should be fetched.

On Monday morning the councillors were taken by barge to Westminster where armed men surrounded the sanctuary. Richard and part of the council retired to the Star Chamber, and the Archbishop of Canterbury and Howard went to the Abbott's quarters to seek the Queen. The Archbishop informed her that force would be used if she refused to release her son, and the grim faces of the lords convinced her.

"I ask for a moment alone with my son," said Bess Woodville.

Lord Howard withdrew with the Archbishop. From the distance he observed her as she knelt and spoke with her child. The boy nodded several times, and several times mother and child embraced. If Howard didn't know Bess's nature, he would have felt a depth of pity for her at this moment. Finally she released her son and watched as he walked away. "Dickon, remember!" she cried plaintively.

The boy turned, tears glistening in his eyes. "I shall remember, my dear lady mother," he said. Then he gave his hand to the Archbishop who led him into the vast empty hall of Westminster Palace where Buckingham awaited to take him to meet Richard.

In the Star Chamber, Richard greeted him affectionately, talked with him for a while, and gave him over to the care of the Archbishop, to be taken to join his brother in the Tower.

The coronation was postponed, Parliament was cancelled. Rumours ran rife in London. The young King was seen with his brother playing ball and shooting arrows on Tower green while whispers said he wouldn't be King much longer. For once, however, there was also good news. There were no disturbances, no demonstrations against Richard in London or anywhere in the land. No lords gathered their retainers and rushed to hide in their castles, and no new plots were discovered. Few knew Richard outside the North, but all knew that in his own region he ruled with a just hand. They were willing to wait. And while they waited, Stillington's secret was disclosed carefully, first to a few, then to more and more. During the week following Hastings's execution, streams of lords, prelates, and influential men of London flowed into Crosby Place and Baynard's Castle to be informed of the pre-contract between King Edward and Lady Eleanor Butler. More and more of these returned to inform the council that they would support Richard's assumption of power.

They would support him. But his mother would not.

Standing on the wall-walk of his mother's castle, Richard looked out at the Thames, inky black in the dead of night. He had written her at length, appraising her of events, of his fears, of the terrible dilemma he found himself in. He had begged for her advice.

Her reply had arrived late that evening. Under no circumstances was he to reveal Edward's pre-contract. Under no circumstances should he accept the throne. She gave no reason.

Why had she urged him against taking the throne? Was it because she knew something no one else knew? *Was he the true son of Richard Plantagenet, Duke of York?* For if he were not, he had no more claim to the throne than his brother's bastards. He looked up at the dark sky. There were no stars, just clouds. He leaned on a parapet, the night breeze stirred his hair. His childhood nightmare had finally forced itself to be examined, weighed, and answered. But only his mother held the answer. How could he ask her? Even if she agreed to come to London, which she had not. That one brief response was all she cared to give. The affairs of this world no longer interested her. Neither the death of her eldest son, nor the torment of her youngest.

The clock at Westminster struck the hour of three. Tomorrow he had promised the council a decision. Wearily, he pushed away from the parapet and made his way down the winding tower steps to his bedchamber, where candles had been left burning for him near the door.

In the dark shadows behind their flickering light, Anne watched Richard. All day—as she went about her business, receiving petitioners, welcoming guests, visiting friends and selecting gifts to be sent to well-wishers—her thoughts had been on him, on what was happening behind the barred doors of Crosby Place and across the way at Baynard's Castle where Richard was to be found more and more. Worried about him, anxious to see him, she had come to Baynard.

She watched as he shut the door gently, careful not to awaken her. Did he really think she could sleep through this misery, when such decisions were being made that would affect the course of their lives? Did he think that by not sharing them with her, he would spare her the agony? She watched as he made his way toward the garderobe. His face was white and haggard, his dark hair in sharp contrast to his pallor. The expression on his face struck at her heart.

Richard lifted his head and saw Anne. He halted in surprise. "My dear love, 'tis late. You should be asleep."

"Nay, my Lord, not on such a night. I've been waiting to know… Have you made a decision?"

He inhaled deeply. "Anne, I have no choice. There is but one decision that can be made. I must take the throne." He attempted a smile, forced a light note into his tone. "Think, my beloved Anne, you shall be Queen of England…"

Swept by black, icy fear, Anne could not move from where she stood. A fierce shivering seized her and her teeth chattered. If she had been handed a sentence of death, she could not have been filled with more terror. Richard went to her, enfolded her into his arms. "My love... my love... you know I don't seek this burden!"

"Then give it up, Richard!" she whispered. "I pray you—for me, for Ned, for us—give it up!"

"Hush, my love... Here, you're cold, take my mantle... Let us sit." He covered her with his crimson cloak and guided her to a silken pallet by the empty fireplace. "I've weighed this from every angle, my love. I do it for the realm, aye, and for myself, so I'm not murdered in my sleep by Woodvilles. But there's one other reason far more compelling to me. It's precisely for you and Ned that I must accept the crown."

He related the dark possibilities and explained how anxiously the lords, prelates, and influential men of the realm supported his accession, viewing it as an urgent necessity for the peace of the realm. As she listened, her uneven breathing became more regular, and her hands, which had been twisting nervously in her lap, gradually stilled. Her shivering eased, and little by little warmth returned to her body.

"I don't know what came over me, Richard, but the thought of being Queen... I suppose it's tied to memories of the past, to my father's failed ambitions for the Crown which rained destruction on us. 'Tis irrational, I know, but I could only think of that night in Caen Castle when my father told me I'd be Queen of England one day. I felt as though I was standing in that room again. It brought back... everything."

"Think not of Caen, my sweet. What has passed is past, and what will come, will come. We shall meet it when it does. But destiny has chosen me—it has offered us a chance to make a better world...We cannot turn away." He pushed back a strand of hair from her pale brow. "I have such dreams for our kingdom, Anne. Edward let the Woodvilles use his power to destroy, and in the end they destroyed him, but we have it in our hands to wield our power for good, to shape a new world. One where no man stands above the law. As in King Arthur's day, Anne... A new Camelot, built on the rule of law."

Behind Richard's head the light of a tapered candle flickered like a star in the night sky, throwing a halo around him. She stared into the deep grey eyes that were filled with his dream. She lifted her hand, traced the cleft in his chin, the line of cheekbone, nose, and jaw. For most of her life, joy had meant this face. She would stand by him, be his helpmate. With God's help, they would find his nights in Camelot.

"Aye, my dear Lord, then so be it," she whispered.

"Fear not, my dearest love," Richard bent his face to hers and gently brushed her lips with his own. "An old archbishop once told me, 'Virtue always prevails.' And he should know, shouldn't he?"

Anne turned her gaze to the candle whose flame seemed to enlarge and brighten all the darkness with its light, and she found herself comforted. Her lips curved into a smile. For the first time in many weeks, the future no longer loomed dark and foreboding, but offered promise.

"'Virtue always prevails,'" she echoed, savouring the words on her lips. "'Tis a good thought, Richard."

Chapter 22

"We sit King, to help the wrong'd."

*B*eneath the hot June sun, the friar mounted the outdoor pulpit at St. Paul's Cross, opened his Bible, looked around the hushed crowd. Then he disclosed the secret of Edward's bigamy.

"Not only did King Edward the Fourth—God assoil his soul—have a pre-contract with Lady Eleanor Butler," he concluded, "but he himself was the bastard son of an archer. Therefore, Richard of Gloucester is the true heir of York and rightful King of England!" He pointed to Richard at the back of the crowd. All eyes turned.

Outraged, Richard stood staring, not at the frowns and tight mouths of enemies and cynics who believed he had concocted the tale in order to usurp his nephew's throne, but at his cousin, Harry, Duke of Buckingham, who had arranged the sermon. He swung on his heel and strode angrily to his stallion. "You had no right!" he fumed to Buckingham under his breath. "No right to proclaim my brother Edward a bastard!"

Buckingham ran to keep up with Richard's furious pace. "I didn't tell them anything they didn't know. When your mother learned of Edward's marriage to Bess, she offered to declare he wasn't the son of your father the Duke, but of an archer, and therefore had no claim to the throne. That's common knowledge."

"And a foul lie, as you well know! You've dishonoured my mother and my brother, and made it look as if it had my blessing! How dare you? From now on you clear everything with me first— *understand?*"

Buckingham's mouth twitched at one corner, and for an instant—so briefly that Richard thought he'd imagined it—his eyes clawed at him like talons. Then the evil look was gone and there remained only the shock of disbelief. Richard's anger ebbed. What was done could not be undone. He owed Buckingham a great deal, and Buckingham was kin, so much like George. In a soft tone, he said, "Harry, I know you've done what you thought best, but it was a mistake. Let us forgive and forget."

After a long moment, Buckingham gave a taut nod. But he averted his eyes so Richard was not able to see if there was forgiveness in them.

Richard put the incident behind him, grateful that Buckingham not only did the same, but even tried to make amends. For three days following the oratory at St. Paul's Cross, his cousin worked hard to gather support by addressing crowds at Westminster, the guildhall, and Parliament. On Thursday, the twenty-sixth day of June, he led a great army of nobles, prelates, and gentry to Baynard's Castle. Richard went to the head of the grand staircase to meet the crowds.

"Lord Protector," Buckingham called in a rousing tone from the foot of the steps, "we have come with a petition! Will you hear us?"

Richard inclined his head.

Buckingham unfurled the parchment grandly. "For the reason of the evils wrought on the land by the Woodvilles..." He read a long list of grievances against the hated clan. Then he began the second charge, "For the reason of the falseness of King Edward's marriage to Elizabeth Woodville..."

Richard listened patiently. He knew each clause by heart, and so did everyone else—they had drafted its words over the past three days.

Buckingham finally came to the end of the list. Only one question remained to be voiced and answered. Raising his silvery voice, Buckingham read, "In consequence, as you are the undoubted son and heir of Richard, late Duke of York, we humbly pray your noble Grace to accept the Crown!"

Richard hesitated. *But am I the undoubted son and heir of Richard, Duke of York?* In the shadows of his mind the fiery dragon of his childhood nightmares reared up and cried, *Thou art no Plantagenet! The Duke of York was not thy father!* He forced the vision away. He had come to the moment of truth and still the truth eluded him. "Is there no one whose claim is before mine?" Richard demanded.

"Lord Protector," called Buckingham with surprise. "You are King Edward's only surviving brother, descended from glorious

Edward III by three of his five sons: by Lionel Duke of Clarence, by John Duke of Lancaster, and by Edmund Duke of York. No one in the land boasts such a claim!"

Time had run out. There could be no more doubt; no more delay. "I accept," said Richard.

A great roar of acclamation burst from a thousand throats as he descended the stairs. "Hail, King Richard III!" they cried. "Hail, most noble King Richard III!"

In the Hall of Rufus at Westminster Palace that same day, Richard sat on his throne. Before him were assembled, at his command, all his judges and lawyers. "As it is my wish that all men should be seen as equal in the eyes of the law, you are ordered to dispense justice without fear or favour," he declared. "Man's justice must reflect God's justice. Abuse of power will not be tolerated and will be dealt with harshly."

He read surprise on many faces. *Aye, it will take time for them to accept such a revolutionary concept*, he thought. Inequality was a fact of life, a trademark of nobility, the underpinning of the feudal system. Many of them, he knew, would not relinquish power readily. "Bring in Sir John Fogge!" he commanded.

There were gasps and shocked murmurs. Richard watched as his deadly enemy, that loathsome relative of the Woodvilles who had played a ruthless role in plundering poor Sir Thomas Cook, was escorted in from Sanctuary. Men peered from behind one another to gain a better view, and Richard heard someone whisper, "Does he mean to hang him?" Fogge's face was indeed ashen pale as if he were going to his death. Richard rose, took him by the hand, and embraced him.

There was a stunned silence.

"This day, past treasons are forgiven and hatreds set aside," said Richard. "I swear to you my friendship, John Fogge, and as evidence of my regard and faith in you, I appoint you Justice of the Peace for the county of Kent."

Applause and cheers shook the hall. Richard smiled. "From this day," he called out in his resonant voice, "I date the first day of my reign. May God bless England!"

Much business awaited Richard. There were decisions to be made regarding the coronation, appointments to be conferred, knighthoods to be bestowed. To the surprise of many, one went to Edward Brampton, though Brampton was born a Jew and had converted to Christianity late in life. But Richard had always believed a man's worth rested on his merits, not on the circumstances of his birth.

There was another task that brought him special pleasure. Righting the wrong done Lord Howard, he raised him to the dukedom of Norfolk, his by hereditary right and stolen by Bess Woodville for her boy, Prince Richard. On the death of Richard's little wife, Anne Mowbray, the earldom had failed to revert to Anne's nearest male kin, John Howard, as it should have. Bess had made sure that the child's marriage contract bore a clause that kept the earldom for her boy. As Richard conferred the coronet on John Howard's silvery head and placed the golden rod into his loyal hands, his mind turned to one now absent, one who had been equally loyal, who had rendered equally hard, faithful service to his King and had been rewarded with malice for his pains. *If only John were here so I could restore into those noble hands the earldom that had meant so much to him!*

Richard watched Howard rise, coronet in place, golden rod in hand. John had been humiliated by his hollow title, forced to live on a pitiful forty pounds a year. That would not happen to Howard. "My good Duke of Norfolk, you are further appointed Admiral of the Seas and granted commissioner of array for the following counties..." He rattled off a third of the counties in England. "You are also granted the yearly income of twenty-three of my royal estates and the manors named herein..." He handed him a charter with a smile.

Howard unfurled the document and gasped. "There must be a hundred manors here, my Lord!"

"No, fair Norfolk. Only fifty."

Howard's eyes glistened. "Thank you, my King."

"'Tis no more than your just due. Would that I could right all such wrongs so easily... *John.*" Richard purposely used the name he had rarely spoken since John's death. There would never be another John, he thought as he embraced Howard, but the Friendly Lion who had escorted him to Middleham on that fateful day long ago was his link with the past, and dear to his heart.

Then Richard turned his mind to the coronation.

"It will be splendid," he said to Anne that night at Baynard's Castle while fires burned outside and drums, flutes, and soldiers' laughter filled the night. "A symbol of what's to come for England. A virtuous court where learning and music flourish and there is justice for the people... Where the church will be led by wise, learned men of true piety. Oh, Anne, I shall give thanks to God daily with my deeds!"

Anne nestled in his arms on the silk-cushioned pallet in his bedchamber, feeling warm and safe, unable to remember what had brought on the attack of shivering fright the previous week. Maybe it was simply her aversion to court. Away from the North, from little Ned, from the calm of Middleham, thrust into the swirl of great events in the making, her health had suffered, leaving her vulnerable to wild imaginings... But Buckingham; was he a wild imagining? What of the hard looks he cast Richard when he thought himself unobserved?

"Richard... about Harry... Is all well between you again—after what he said about Edward, I mean?"

"Aah, Harry... Harry's well meaning, but he can be rash at times. And harm's been done, for certain... I find it strange, Anne, that a body can heal from all but the deepest cut, sometimes without a scar, yet a man's reputation, once injured by words, never truly recovers." Richard mulled his own words thoughtfully. "Never mind, my sweet, we've made peace. Harry's remorseful and has written my lady mother an apology. I, in turn, have entrusted him with the arrangements for our coronation."

Anne wished she shared Richard's confidence in their cousin Buckingham, but the reassurance left her more unsettled than ever. *Buckingham*...

With a determined effort, she drove Buckingham from her mind. This was a happy time; she mustn't spoil it with dismal thoughts.

As Richard had said, what will come, will come, but whatever happened, they had been given a chance to shape the future. With God's grace, they would leave the world a better place.

From the crook of his arm, she stole a look at his face, dim in the candlelight. *It was the right decision to take the throne,* she thought. Richard would make a noble king, possibly the finest England had ever known, for he bore all the markings. She rose, went to the coffer, and took out the lute. At his side again, she strummed the chords of their "Song of the North" that Richard had composed for her as they stood admiring the twilight at Barnard Castle in that unforgettably sweet first month of their marriage.

"Sing with me, Richard... *Aye, O, aye—the winds that bend the brier! The winds that blow the grass!*"

Richard joined his deep tenor to her sweet voice. *"For the time was May-time and blossoms draped the earth..."*

End of Book Two

Author's Note

This book is historical fiction based on real people of the period and real events. No characters have been invented, and I have adhered to historical facts when these are known. Time, place, and character have not been manipulated, and the actual words known to have been used by the historical figures represented here have been integrated into the story whenever possible. However, details that cannot be historically verified are the product of my imagination.

For the ease of the modern reader, the quotations used come from Tennyson's *Idylls of the King,* not from Sir Thomas Malory's *Morte d'Arthur,* written in Richard's lifetime.

One question I have been asked with some frequency regards Anne's vegetarianism. It may come as a surprise to many that there were, indeed, vegetarians in the fifteenth century. This fact is documented by John Stowe in *Stowe's Survey of London,* which has been regarded as the prime authority on the history of London from its initial publication in 1598.[1] Stowe reports that at a Christmas feast in the ninth year of Henry VII's reign, sixty dishes were served to the Queen, Elizabeth of York, none of which were "fish or flesh."

As to Richard's deformity, no one who knew him during his lifetime ever mentioned one. The Countess of Desmond, who danced with Richard at a banquet, is reported to have said that he was the handsomest young man in the room besides his brother the King. Shakespeare's immortal image of the limping hunchback with the withered arm shouting, "A horse, a horse, my kingdom for a horse!" is also disputed by Richard's surviving portrait, thought to have been painted from life or copied from a contemporary painting, which shows a handsome, well-formed young man.[2] Other facts that dispute the hunchback image will be presented in *Fall From Grace,* the third, and final book in *The Rose of York* series.

The reader may be interested to learn that no information exists as to the identity of the woman, or women, who bore Richard's two illegitimate children. I have taken Rosemary Horrox's suggestion that it was Katherine Haute.[3] It is known that the children came to live with Richard at an early age, and when I came across a reference to his vast generosity to the Benedictine nunnery of St. Mary in Barking, Essex, which has puzzled historians, the reason suggested itself to me.[4]

Proof of Edward's bigamy has failed to survive the centuries. This is not surprising, however, in view of the fact that Henry Tudor went to great lengths to destroy evidence that conflicted with his account of events. Richard's bloodless accession, his explicit inclusion of Edward's troth-plight in his Parliament of 1484 when a generalization would have sufficed, and Henry Tudor's subsequent relentless efforts to pervert or suppress mention of it, testifies to the truth of Stillington's revelation and suggests that such evidence existed, and that it proved persuasive.

Regarding a final and critical question: Was Richard III a hero, or a villain?

Most modern historians accept that the origin of Shakespeare's portrait of Richard III lies in Tudor propaganda. However, by the end of the sixteenth century, Tudor propaganda had become historical fact.

After every conflict the victor rewrites history, and Henry Tudor was no exception. Having won the throne by right of conquest, he set a dangerous precedent for his own future. The legend of the hideous, villainous monster was deliberately initiated during his reign in order to justify his usurpation. He hired an Italian historian, Polydore Vergil, to paint his predecessor as evil and forge his propaganda into history. Sir Thomas More absorbed the Tudor version from Richard's old enemy, Bishop Morton, in whose household he was reared as a child, but More neither finished, nor published, his account of Richard's reign. The manuscript was discovered by his nephew fifteen years after his death, and translated from the Latin. Published posthumously, it was taken up by Tudor historians Hall and Holinshed. Shakespeare's play sealed the legend. As soon as the last Tudor lay dead, the people of the North rallied to right the injustice done to Richard's memory. George Buck was the first, then came Horace Walpole. With his book *Historic Doubts*, Walpole created a debate that rages to this day and includes both historians and novelists.

S.W.

Endnotes

1. *Stowe's Survey of London*, (Introduction by H.E. Wheatley); Everyman's Library, Dutton, New York; p. 415

2. There is evidence that Richard's only surviving portrait was doctored to give him uneven shoulders.

3. Rosemary Horrox, *Richard III: A Study of Service*; Cambridge University Press, 1989; p. 81

4. Charles Ross, *Richard III*; University of California Press, 1981; p. 130

The day dawned brilliant with sunshine for the first double coronation in two hundred years. At the hour of Prime, as church bells pealed across London, with Anne's train following his, Richard of Gloucester left Westminster Hall for the crowning at the Abbey. Removing his shoes, he walked barefoot on the red carpet, heralds trumpeting the way, followed by his lords and a procession of priests, abbots, bishops, and a cardinal bearing a great cross high over his head.

Richard's gaze fell on ginger-bearded Lord Stanley carrying the mace. He remembered his own words: *One thing men can rely on, as surely as spring follows winter—a Stanley will ride at the winner's side, no matter what his sin.* He hadn't intended to reward Stanley for his treason, yet he had. To appease his own guilt for taking the life of a better man, he supposed, wincing at the memory of Lord Hastings. Even Stanley's wife, Margaret Beaufort, had been greatly honoured this day. Harry Buckingham, a good friend and cousin, whom he'd entrusted with the coronation, had arranged for her to carry Anne's train—she, the mother of Henry Tudor, who, now that all true Lancastrian claimants were dead, had become their claimant merely because he lived! The world was indeed a strange place.

Richard wondered how Anne fared. Suffering from a chill and fever on the previous day, she'd been carried in a litter for the traditional journey of the monarch from the Tower of London to Westminster Palace. Much to his relief, she had felt well enough this morning to walk in the ceremony, and now followed him into Westminster Abbey. At least this once the wagging tongues that sought evil omens would be stilled.

No one would have guessed she had been so ill, for she looked beautiful in her crimson velvet mantle furred with miniver and her fair hair flowing down her back, giving no hint of her recent illness. His sister Liza walked behind her, trailed by more noble ladies and a line of knights. His eldest sister, Nan, however, was absent. Of course his mother had not come. She had even refused her blessing. He forced the memory away. But the entire peerage of England was here. That was much to be grateful for. It meant that England accepted him with good heart.

They approached the west door of the Abbey. The sign of the Red Pale in the courtyard of the almonry swung in the breeze. Here, in 1476, William Caxton, that old mercer of Bruges, had come to print his books with the help of the Gutenberg press that he'd brought from Germany. It was a long way they'd travelled together since that wintry afternoon in the Bruges tavern, Richard thought, marvelling at the caprices of life. He'd been a youth of seventeen then, broken-hearted, hungry, and poor, an exile from the land of his birth with little hope. Now he would be King.

His gaze moved from Caxton's shop to his friend Francis Lovell carrying the Sword of Justice, and he remembered a question Francis had posed when they were boys. "If you could be anyone in King Arthur's court, who would you be?" He'd had no answer then. Lancelot, whom he'd admired as the embodiment of his valiant cousin John Neville, had seemed out of reach to him. Later, torn between love and loyalty, he had felt himself more like Lancelot than any of Arthur's knights, for Lancelot had been the most flawed.

I can answer you at last, Francis, he thought. *I shall be Arthur, reigning with mercy and justice.*

~*~

The high, pure voices of the choristers lifted in praise. Song burst forth from the church: *Domine in virtute...*

Richard and Anne entered the nave and proceeded down the aisle. Hundreds of candles flickered and incense ladened the air with a rich, heavy scent, sending curls of smoke wafting into the gloomy nave. At the high altar, Anne watched as Richard knelt to be anointed with the holy Chrism, and rose to be vested in his regal garments of black and gold. Girded with the sword of state, he knelt again. Old Cardinal Bourchier picked up the Crown of St. Edward and set it down on his head.

From the corner of her eye, Anne saw Richard's cousin Harry

PRAISE FOR *NON-OBVIOUS*

"*Non-Obvious* is a sharp, articulate, and immediately useful book about one of my favorite topics: the future. Filled with actionable advice and entertaining stories, Rohit offers an essential guidebook to using the power of curation to understand and prepare for the future of business."

—DANIEL H. PINK
Author of *To Sell Is Human* and *Drive*

"Shatter your magic crystal ball, and toss out the tea leaves. In this book, Rohit shows us how and where to find the future trends that will shape your business, your brand, and even your own decision-making."

—SALLY HOGSHEAD
NY Times bestselling author of *How The World Sees You*

"There are very few books that I read hoping that no one else around me will. They're the books that are so insightful, so thought provoking and so illuminating that they provide powerful competitive advantage. *Non-Obvious* is one of those. Pass on it at your own peril."

—SHIV SINGH
SVP Global Head of Digital & Marketing Transformation at VISA
and author of *Social Media Marketing For Dummies*

"*Non-Obvious* should be called *oblivious* since that's how you'll be if this book isn't on your shelf. I actually wish some of Rohit's predictions won't come true ('Selfie Confidence'!? Nooo!) ... but usually they do. He's the best at this, and this book shows you why."

—SCOTT STRATTEN
Four-time best-selling author, including 2014 Sales Book of the Year: *UnSelling*

"This is one of those rare books that delivers insights that are both useful and help illuminate where business is going. It's a great read."

—CHARLES DUHIGG
Author of the bestseller *The Power Of Habit*

"For the last four years, Rohit has helped make the non-obvious obvious by spotlighting trends to help anyone prepare their business for the future. It gets better every year so if you haven't been reading, it's time to start."

—RYAN HOLIDAY
Author of *Trust Me I'm Lying* and *Growth Hacker Marketing*

"The aim of many business books is to give a man a fish. Rohit generously goes one better—not by simply telling us what's working, but by showing us how to apply his thinking for ourselves."

—BERNADETTE JIWA
Bestselling author, award-winning blogger & keynote speaker

"Rohit Bhargava's "Likeonomics" is the gold standard on understanding the social economy. His new book had me at "predict the future" but there's much more than that in here. It's about seeing the world in a new way — plus a powerful argument for how curation can change your organization."

—SREE SREENIVASAN
Chief Digital Officer, The Metropolitan Museum of Art Host,
"@Sree Show" podcast on CBS @Playit network

"Rohit provides a goldmine of ideas and trends that will shape the future of marketing and product development. Read this book to get in front of the herd."

—GUY KAWASAKI
Chief Evangelist of Canva
Author of *The Art of the Start, 2.0*

"Seeing things that others don't is perhaps the highest form of creativity that exists. Unlock the Non-Obvious approach and you can write your ticket to success in any field."

—JOHN JANTSCH
Author of *Duct Tape Marketing* and *Duct Tape Selling*

Rohit Bhargava collects ideas the way frequent fliers collect miles. His infectious enthusiasm for trends and strategy is a recipe for success for your enterprise. In *Non Obvious*, he provides the solution to a problem business owners, entrepreneurs, heads of marketing, and CEOs have struggled with for years —how do you identify where the market is headed and be there first, ready to take advantage of it. Artfully lacing stories together to pull out simple, yet powerful trends, Rohit offers a blueprint for making trend identification a key component of your business strategy. The format of his book makes it easy for the novice to adopt these principles, and for the expert to glean pearls of wisdom. While the title is Non Obvious, your next step should be obvious —read this book today!

—JOEY COLEMAN
Chief Experience Composer at Design Symphony

"Lots of books tell you to "think different" but *Non-Obvious* is one of the few books that actually teaches you how to do it. Whether you are trying to persuade clients, motivate a team, or just impress a demanding boss —*Non-Obvious* can help you succeed. I've already purchased copies for my entire team."

—JOHN GERZEMA
New York Times best-selling author and social strategist

"Very few people understand the world of digital business better than Rohit and I have introduced my clients to his ideas for years. His new book is a must-read resource for learning to see patterns, anticipate global trends, and think like a futurist every day!"

—GERD LEONHARD
Author and keynote speaker Basel / Switzerland

"It doesn't take a crystal ball to predict that digital is the future. Rather than tell you what you already know, Rohit sets his sights on something much more important: helping you adopt a more curious and observant mindset to understand the world around you. If you believe in a lifetime of learning, read this book!"

—JONATHAN BECHER
Chief Marketing Officer, SAP